# Not Not Normal

PETER E. FENTON

JAMES LORIMER & COMPANY LTD., PUBLISHERS
TORONTO

James Lorimer & Company Ltd., Publishers acknowledges funding support from the Ontario Arts Council (OAC), an agency of the Government of Ontario. We acknowledge the support of the Canada Council for the Arts. This project has been made possible in part by the Government of Canada and with the support of Ontario Creates.

Cover design: Tyler Cleroux
Cover image: Shutterstock

Library and Archives Canada Cataloguing in Publication

Title: Not not normal / Peter E. Fenton.
Names: Fenton, Peter E., author.
Series: RealLove.
Description: Series statement: Real love
Identifiers: Canadiana (print) 20240321987 | Canadiana (ebook) 20240322061 | ISBN 9781459419322 (hardcover) | ISBN 9781459419315 (softcover) | ISBN 9781459419339 (EPUB)
Subjects: LCGFT: Novels.
Classification: LCC PS8611.E577 N68 2024 | DDC jC813/.6—dc23

Published by:
James Lorimer &
Company Ltd., Publishers
117 Peter Street, Suite 304
Toronto, ON, Canada
M5V 0M3
www.lorimer.ca

Distributed in Canada by:
Formac Lorimer Books
5502 Atlantic Street
Halifax, NS, Canada
B3H 1G4
www.formaclorimerbooks.ca

Distributed in the US by:
Lerner Publisher Services
241 1st Ave. N.
Minneapolis, MN, USA
55401
www.lernerbooks.com

Printed and bound in Canada.

*For the* real *Mr. (David) Jenkins.*

# 01 Today's Insta Post

JORDAN LAID OUT TWO PADS OF PAPER, two pens, two pencils (sharpened), and one green and one blue highlighter. Glasses were set out for water on his desk — the meeting was going to be in Jordan's bedroom, and he only allowed water in there. It was 8:30 in the morning and Emma was due at nine to have a planning session for tomorrow, the first day of Grade Eleven at Playter Heights Secondary School.

He looked at everything. Something wasn't right.

First, he straightened the pens. It still didn't feel right, so he replaced the pencils with two that were the same length. Still not . . . It was the highlighters — "No! Stop it right now," he whispered. Jordan quickly pushed everything out of order.

For a full minute, he stared at the visual chaos, then without thinking, straightened one pen, then another, then the pads of paper until everything was as tidy as before. He sighed. Was he ever going to be normal? That's all he ever wanted, ever dreamed of — NOT to be a freak.

The phone rang with a double chirp indicating a call from the intercom at the front door. Mr. Swan, the daytime doorman, must have been away from his desk. He usually let Emma in without question. Jordan buzzed her in. He thought about when they had first met. He'd transferred to Playter Heights Secondary School in grade nine and had found himself being regularly bullied for being small, quiet, and the new kid in the school. Jordan remembered cowering as he was surrounded by a taunting mass of bigger kids, then the sound of a single, high-pitched yell followed by the screams of the boys in the crowd. Jordan had looked up when the yelling started and spotted a skinny girl with carrot-orange hair, grinning wildly. The braces on her teeth had gleamed in the sunlight as she'd cut through the crowd on her inline skates, weaving in and out and running into as many toes as she could. In that moment Jordan and Emma had become the closest of friends, and Emma had become his protector.

There was a knock on the apartment door, and Jordan heard Emma let herself in.

"Good morning, Mr. Shepherd," she called out to Jordan's dad.

"Hello, Emma," his dad called back from the living room. Jordan knew he'd be on the sofa finishing the crossword in yesterday's newspaper.

Jordan met Emma in the hallway that led to his bedroom. "Morning!" she said, giving him a hug.

She always hugged him, even though he shuddered when she did. He thought Emma did it on purpose. Jordan wasn't a touchy-feely kind of person.

"Come on," he said, prying himself away from her, then headed down the hall to his bedroom, a space where every wall was covered in neatly shelved books.

Emma stood at the door of the bedroom, pulled out her phone, and took a picture of the school supplies on Jordan's bed.

"What are you doing?" he asked.

"Just a second," she said. "There. Today's Insta post. 'Let the school games begin!'"

"Wait. You posted a picture of my bed?"

"Don't worry," she said, reaching over and rubbing his shoulder. "I didn't say whose it was. Look, if I don't post something every day, I'll lose followers. You know how it is."

Jordan had no idea how it was. He had Snapchat, Instagram, and TikTok accounts — all set up for him by Emma — but he never posted on any of them. What would he say? Besides, Emma was his only follower and he could just tell her what he wanted her to know without going through the bother of posting it for the world to see.

As they sat down on the bed, the carefully laid-out meeting supplies shifted. The pens and pencils rolled out of place. Jordan immediately reorganized them, but they rolled away again. As he reached for them Emma touched his hand. "Maybe we should sit on the floor."

"Right."

They moved off of the bed and Jordan got the pencils and pens safely lined up, just the way he liked them.

"First off, this year we have to change the name of the group," Jordan said.

"And that's important, why?" Emma asked.

"No one is going to sign up for a book club called Bookwormers. It sounds like a parasitic infection."

"It's a high school. No one is going to sign up for it no matter what it's called."

"The book club *has* members," Jordan protested.

"Four of us. It's not so much a club as a . . . casual gathering."

"And it won't grow if we don't have an exciting name."

"What would make a book club exciting?" Emma asked.

"Latin," he said, with confidence.

Emma thought for a minute. "You mean like Erick Brian Colón?"

"Who?"

"That hot Latino singer from CNCO . . ."

Jordan just stared at her.

"It's a boy band . . ." She reached for her phone. "I could play you something of theirs."

Jordan crossed his arms. "I said Latin, like the language. Not Latino, like your singer."

Emma frowned. "Well, you're never gonna find a date if you think Latin is sexy."

"I said exciting, not . . . sexy, and that's why I propose we ask the school to rename the book club . . . X-Libris." He held up a sign that he'd run off on his printer.

Emma said nothing.

"It would be like a play on 'Ex Libris' . . . You know, like on book plates."

Emma looked lost.

Jordan grabbed one of his mother's books off of the shelf and opened it to the inside cover. He showed her a printed sticker that read EX LIBRIS JANICE FRANCO. "It means 'From the library of Janice Franco'. That was my mother's name before she got married. I was thinking of changing the name of the club to X-Libris, like — from the library. Like a book's been liberated from one person's private collection. We'll be setting the words free and into the world!" Jordan was excited.

Emma continued to just stare at him.

"What? It's pretty . . . dope!" he said.

"When you say that, it doesn't sound right."

"Okay. Cool, then."

"You, my adorably nerdy friend, have no idea what cool is, do you?"

"Well, X-Libris is better than Bookwormers! We might even get picked on less. And we may be able to expand our membership."

"From four."

"Who knows — by the end of the year we could have . . . five!"

"Well, I think you should make your case to the school librarian first thing tomorrow morning. Tell him just what you told me. I think you can convince him."

"Maybe *you* could ask him?" Jordan said hopefully.

Emma shook her head. "No! Now, let's get out of here. I'm taking you out for coffee. It's our last day of freedom before school starts."

Jordan hesitated. "I don't feel . . ."

"You'll be fine," Emma said. "And you'll be fine tomorrow. Now come on, let's go."

# 02 The Boy in the Mirror

AT THE FRONT DOOR TO THE APARTMENT, Jordan put his shoes on, double-tying his laces. As he waited for Emma, who had gone to say goodbye to his father, Jordan looked at himself in the mirror. A thin boy with light brown hair and hazel-coloured eyes stared back. Jordan raised his eyebrows to greet him. The boy in the mirror greeted him back. The boy wasn't that bad-looking. He'd grown taller over the summer. He'd reached almost 180 centimetres, and he'd gained some muscle on his lean frame. Jordan wondered if the mirror boy was called "freak" as often as Jordan was. Maybe the mirror was a nicer place to live in.

"Ready?" Emma said. Jordan was startled to see her standing beside him. She reached over and fixed his hair, then pulled him out the door.

As they walked the ten minutes to Playter Perk, the most popular coffee shop in the neighbourhood, Emma said, "Your dad seems a lot better."

"I guess," Jordan replied. "I wish he'd talk more about Mom."

"I think some people react differently than others. I'm sure he misses her as much as you do." She squeezed his hand and then said, "Come on. Let's get you something to drink."

In spite of Emma's insistence that he should try coffee for a change, Jordan ordered his usual: a tea. Still, to please Emma he ordered Earl Grey. He thought it would be more celebratory given this was the last day of vacation. Emma had a vanilla sweet cream cold brew with a caramel shot. She sat across from him sipping her drink.

"So . . . I've been thinking . . ." she started.

"No," Jordan said, shaking his head.

"But you don't know what I'm going to say."

Jordan took a sip of his tea and gave her a hard stare, meaning *Don't.* At the same time, he reached over and straightened her spoon.

She gently touched his hand. "I think it would be good for you to . . . work at getting past some of your habits. It's time to gain some confidence. Maybe even find someone to go on a date with. You're sort of cute. Heck, I'd even consider dating you if I wasn't your friend, and you didn't prefer boys."

"We agreed not to talk about that unless I brought it up first."

"But you do like guys."

"I know I do," Jordan said in a hushed tone, "but now's not the time for me to think about it. I've got enough challenges to deal with, without adding dating someone to the list."

Emma leaned closer to him. "What is it that's

really bothering you?"

Jordan squirmed. "It's not that I'm totally against it. I'd like a boyfriend but . . . what if I fall for a guy and he's not into me? Or worse, I fall for someone who's not gay or even bi and I tell them how I feel. I could get beaten up. And what if I find someone I like and I have one of my attacks in front of them? The whole thing just scares me."

"Dating is scary, but it's the start of a new year and anything is possible. Even for you."

"And why is the beginning of the year different than any other time?"

"Because people have had a whole summer to forget the old you —"

Jordan looked up then and saw a tall muscular boy looming above him. "Freak!" the boy said and flicked the top of Jordan's head before ambling away.

"They never forget," Jordan muttered, rubbing his head.

"Ignore him," Emma said. "Brody was in math class with me last year. If it's not sports, he doesn't believe in it." She pulled out her phone. "Look over here. Now lean in," she said, spinning around and taking a picture of the two of them. "This selfie marks the official beginning of Jordan's year of change." She showed him the photo. Emma was smiling her huge smile. Jordan's face had his usual bewildered look, and Brody was standing behind them, his middle finger raised.

"Change makes me nervous. Isn't it enough that we're heading into a different grade?" Jordan asked.

Emma said nothing. She just shifted the camera the other way so that it was only the two of them in the frame and snapped another picture. She posted it and then said, "Trust me, change can be a good thing. I just have a feeling that this is going to be your year."

# 03 A Monster Under the Bed

JORDAN CLOSED THE BOOK he was reading and tried to sleep. It was late and he couldn't stop thinking about what Emma had said that morning about it being his year — about things changing. The last time that things had changed it had involved, well, just about everything. Jordan thought back to the 'before times' in the nice house on the peaceful street near High Park. He was an only child, which had suited him just fine. He hadn't had many friends so he'd spent hours reading books and writing fantasy stories in his room. *The Swordsman's Destiny* was his favourite. It was a tale of a man who found true love by overcoming a series of challenges. It was the last story he had written before . . .

Jordan loved stories. His mother had made a ritual of reading to Jordan every day. Her love of reading had poured off of her and onto him like rain. And, like rain on his clothes, it had soaked in. When he was really young she had read to him just before nap time and again before bed. He later found out that those daytime naps were as much for her as for him. She had needed the rest.

Two years ago, when Jordan had just turned fourteen, his mother passed away after losing her war with cancer. Jordan had felt numbed by the loss. He remembered crying a lot and clutching the last book she had read to him, Isaac Asimov's *Pebble in the Sky*. He had carried it everywhere he went. Even to her funeral.

Jordan also remembered how things with his father

had changed. His father used to be more confident but now he seemed . . . uncertain. Jordan's mom had been the organized one, making sure that meals were prepared and keeping track of the family's finances. Since she'd been gone Jordan and his dad had been muddling through, but there was an awkwardness to it all.

Aunt Judith, his father's sister, had told Jordan to just give him time. "He's not used to doing the job of two parents. He's just trying his best to figure it all out." She had come to stay with them for a while, primarily to make sure the two men of the house ate something.

Jordan recalled overhearing a conversation between his father and aunt. In the end, the two decided that Jordan's dad would sell the house and start fresh. His dad seemed committed to the idea. When he'd told Jordan the plan, saying it would be best for everyone, Jordan had yelled "By everyone, you mean YOU, don't you?" Jordan didn't want to leave the place where he had made so many memories with his mother.

The fights that ensued did nothing to change

the plan, and in six months they had moved into the apartment. Jordan might not have gotten his way, but he was determined to save his mother's books.

"But, Jordan — we have no room for all of them," his father had protested.

"They can stay with me in my room," Jordan had said, like they were puppies that he'd found on the doorstep. Jordan saved the memory of his mother, in the form of her collection of books, and moved into the largest of the apartment's two bedrooms which now resembled a library with a small bed in the corner.

It was around that time that he'd first noticed himself changing. His habits had gotten worse. He needed to have more control over his world, which had shifted so much. He needed everything to be organized. When things were organized, they could be relied on. They were . . . safer.

His doctor had prescribed him a pill that was supposed to help him to not "lose it" — Jordan's words for what the doctor called a panic attack. The word *panic* didn't even come close to what he felt.

It started with a gnawing feeling in his stomach . . . that feeling you have when you think there's a monster under your bed, but you're too afraid to check. And then his heart would start to pound and he couldn't breathe, like the invisible monster was standing on his chest. Logically he knew there was no monster, but somewhere inside his mind, there was a short circuit that put him in a state of terror.

Having an attack at home was bad enough, but at school . . . well, it wasn't something you ever lived down. Jordan thought about the morning he'd realized that he couldn't remember the sound of his mother's voice. It was like she'd died all over again. All of a sudden, the air had been sucked out of the school. He hadn't been able to breathe. Jordan had run through the halls. He knew he had to get outside. He was crying so hard he couldn't see where he was going and ran right into another student. The guy had looked at him and started to laugh. A few others had joined in. The words "Freak!" and "Baby" still rang through his head. Jordan couldn't allow that to ever happen again.

So, he'd tried what the doctor had recommended. The pills sometimes helped, but mostly just slowed down his brain and made him feel like he was tired all the time. Jordan and his dad had agreed to have the doctor take him off the pills. Instead, he was then sent to a therapist who gave him some exercises to help calm himself down. This also worked . . . sometimes, but when things got out of control, he needed to get himself to a safe space where he could be alone. Jordan's biggest fear was that he would lose control at school again. The possibility gave him that gnawing feeling — *the monster is coming for you Jordan . . . STOP IT!*

Jordan knew he wasn't going to get to sleep. He calmed his breathing, reached for his mother's favourite book, and started at the beginning again, for what seemed like the hundredth time.

# 04 New Year, New Beginnings

IT WAS HIS FIRST DAY BACK, and by the time Jordan reached the school, Emma was already waiting for him at the fence beside the entrance.

"New year, new beginnings. Right?" she said.

"Right," Jordan said. He pretended her pep-talks helped. In his heart, he really didn't believe it, but she meant well and he appreciated her attempts to support him.

"Things can change if you want them to," she added.

But the fact was Jordan hated change. He hated that his mom had died. He hated that they had moved. He hated that he'd had to start at a new school. Too many changes. He wanted things to be like they used to be, but that wasn't going to happen today because on the first day of a new school year, everything was different. Welcome to Grade Eleven.

Jordan arrived at his homeroom and scouted it out. He didn't spot anyone that was an obvious threat, like Brody.

Mr. Banks, who usually taught gym, was Jordan's homeroom teacher. He always wore a tight-fitting t-shirt with a University of Guelph logo. That and a pair of tight shorts or sweatpants, depending on the weather. The pants had the same logo. Mr. Banks was obviously very proud that he had worked for The University of Guelph. He was always quick to mention that he had been the coach of their football team.

*Then what horrible thing happened that made you stoop to teaching high school?* Jordan wondered.

Mr. Banks started with the first-day announcements

and warnings. As he was taking attendance, a new student entered. The student apologized for being late and said they'd lost his records in the office. He handed Mr. Banks a note which the teacher glanced at, then said, "Okay, Tremblay, find a seat at the back."

Jordan watched as the student made his way to the back of the class. The kid's pack was almost as big as he was and he bumped into everything around him. He knocked Jordan's desk and sent his neatly laid out pens spiralling.

"Sorry about that," he said, glancing at Jordan as he passed. The boy's eyes were the most remarkable jade green colour. They only made eye contact for a few seconds, but Jordan felt a strange tingle in the pit of his stomach.

*What the. . .?*

Jordan told his stomach to shut up and he started to straighten his pens. Maybe it was the fact that the kid was late or the chaos he brought that didn't sit well with Jordan. Or maybe it was something else. His discomfort was short-lived. The bell rang and he got up and headed off to his first class, French.

Madame Choix's French class was on the second floor. As Jordan walked up the second flight of steps he heard someone moving quickly behind him. As the person passed him, their elbow jutted out and hit Jordan hard in the arm, sending his books flying.

"Spaz," Brody snarled. "You are such a goddamn loser."

Jordan's heart pounded. *Not now,* he thought frantically. *Not on the first day of school!*

He focused on his breathing. Air in through the nose, out through the mouth. In through the nose. Out through the mouth.

As Brody walked away, a girl Jordan had never met before helped him pick up his books. "That guy's got problems," was all she said. Jordan just stood there as she loaded books back into his arms.

★★★

Jordan made it through French and Math without incident, and then decided to play it safe and avoid the cafeteria at lunch. Instead, he took the sandwich he'd made that morning down to Mr. Jenkins's office.

Jordan remembered meeting Mr. Jenkins on his first day of high school. A group of older boys had spotted Jordan neatly organizing and then reorganizing his cutlery, plate, and cup on the table in the cafeteria. When their insults had turned physical, Jordan had run away from them and found safety in a dark, basement room. The room was a disturbing mess of clutter, but hiding there had seemed better than being beaten up.

A voice had come out of the dark. "Can I help you?" Jordan was frozen in terror until he'd seen a slightly stooped older man with a friendly face sitting in a chair underneath a window. Jordan recognized him as the caretaker who swept the hallway floors. "Come for a bit of peace and quiet?"

Jordan nodded.

"Here," the caretaker had said, pointing to another chair beside his desk. "Have a seat and join me for lunch." After that day, lunch with Mr. Jenkins had become a several-day-a-week thing. In time they had become friends.

Jordan was glad to see Mr. Jenkins sitting at his desk when he got to the caretaker's office. Nothing had changed since last year.

"Good afternoon, Mr. Jenkins," Jordan said.

"Well, welcome back. I hope you had a nice summer."

"It was okay, thanks. And you?" Jordan asked.

"Not bad as well. So, Grade Eleven is it?"

"Yup. Mind if I join you?"

"No problem," Mr. Jenkins said, making room for Jordan's lunchtime setup.

The nice thing about having lunch with Mr. Jenkins was that the caretaker rarely spoke, and he never tried to shove your face in your tuna sandwich.

Jordan ate in silence and, after he'd finished, said, "Nice to see you again."

Mr. Jenkins just nodded his head as Jordan made his way to his afternoon classes.

★★★

The first day at school had gone surprisingly well. There had been no disasters, if you didn't include the encounter with Brody in the stairwell. Before Jordan left for home, he had one more thing he needed to do, and that was to go and see Mr. Childs, the school librarian.

All of the school's clubs had a staff supervisor. The supervisors didn't have to take part in any club activities, or even attend any of their meetings. They were just supposed to be available to handle any problems or to provide the students with supplies if they needed them. Mr. Childs was the book club's staff supervisor. Jordan knew he would have to get his permission to change the name of the club.

He made his way to the second-floor library and entered. Inside the door, he saw Mr. Childs sitting at his desk in the reading room. Jordan froze. *What's the worst he can say to me? No! Don't think that.* Jordan took three deep breaths, but he didn't feel any less frightened. So, he took a bunch more. Enough that he felt dizzy. He staggered a bit.

"Are you all right over there?" Mr. Childs called

out. "Should I call the school nurse?"

"No. I'm all right."

Jordan weaved his way to Mr. Childs's desk. He felt so worried that when he opened his mouth to speak, all that came out was a faint whisper. Mr. Childs, who had gone back to reading a book, looked up.

"Speak up. I know it's a library, but I can't make out a word you're saying."

Jordan breathed in and in one breath said, "Mr. Childs, you probably don't remember me but my name is Jordan Shepherd and I'm the president of the student book club and I was hoping that I could convince you to let us change the name of the book club and I feel, in all honesty, that the current name, Bookwormers, is —"

"You can call it whatever you want. Frankly, I don't care."

"I was thinking of . . . X-Libris? . . ." Jordan said, expecting that his idea would be shot down in flames.

"Sounds perfectly inoffensive. Now, if there's

nothing else . . ."

"No, sir. That's it!" Jordan was ecstatic. His first major decision since he'd come to school this year had been accepted by the school administration, or its representative at least. He had triumphed!

Jordan realized that for some people this wouldn't be a big deal, but for him, he had done something major and nothing bad had happened. Maybe Emma was right. Maybe this would be his year.

# 05 The Great Upheaval

LIKE THAT MORNING, EMMA WAS LEANING up against the fence waiting for Jordan when he left the school.

"So, how did it go? I don't see any scars or blood," she said.

Jordan shook his head. "I got the name change passed by Mr. Childs, but I was insanely nervous."

"You took a step. I'm proud of you," she said, throwing her arms around him in a hug which he immediately squirmed out of. "Jeez, it's like trying to hug a cat."

They walked part way home together. Emma joked about gym class. Jordan said the closest he got to gym was Mr. Banks in homeroom.

"Was it shorts or track pants today?" she asked.

"Shorts," he said, grinning.

"Oooh, I bet you liked that," she said, poking him in the ribs.

"Shut up." Jordan felt himself blushing. He decided to change the subject. "A new kid showed up in homeroom. He was like *five minutes late!*"

"Wow. Five whole minutes?"

Jordan decided to ignore the sarcasm. "And he wore a huge backpack. I swear it must have held everything he owned."

"Huh. What did he look like?"

"Uh . . . I don't really remember. He was kinda slim. Oh, and he had the most amazing green eyes." *And curly jet-black hair and pale skin.*

Jordan must have been standing there silent for a while because Emma shook his shoulder and said, "Earth to Jordan. Come in, Jordan."

"Sorry," he said. "Must have zoned out."

Emma tilted her head and smirked. "Sure. Look, I've gotta go. See you tomorrow." She started to head off, then turned. "And congratulations again on getting the name of the book club changed." She gave him a quick hug and then walked away, leaving him standing there, grinning.

*I'm going to love Grade Eleven.*

Jordan stopped by the Shop 'n' Bag convenience store and picked up his dad's paper on his way home. He'd started doing this when they moved to the apartment. Jordan noticed that spending time with the previous day's paper each morning seemed to comfort his father. It wasn't the news that he cared about. He could get up-to-date news online whenever he wanted. It was the crossword puzzle. His dad and mom always used to sit at the table after breakfast and work on the puzzle together. It was a happy ritual. Rituals were routines, and Jordan understood the importance of being able to count on routine. For both his dad and him.

The move had been a chaotic time for the two of them. His dad had taken a leave of absence from working at the vet clinic as he arranged for what Jordan later called The Great Upheaval. Jordan knew that when his dad had started back to work, he'd reduced his clinic hours so he could always be there when Jordan got home from school . . . just in case Jordan needed him.

As Jordan entered his apartment building, he looked at the doorman. Jordan thought he looked like he was at least eighty years old. Apparently, he'd been the daytime doorman at the Belvedere Apartments for fifty years. "I hope your day went well, Mr. Swan."

"Fairly well, Jordan. And how was your first day at school?"

"Perfect," he said, knocking on Mr. Swan's desk like it would bring him continued luck.

"Glad to hear it," Mr. Swan replied. "Oh, this arrived for your father about half an hour ago." He passed Jordan a padded envelope.

Jordan looked at the return address. It had been forwarded from where they used to live. Mail was still being sent to his old house. His heart sank. The envelope would probably contain something addressed to his mother and if his father saw it, it would only upset him. Jordan would open it himself when he got upstairs.

Inside the apartment he found his dad, sitting on the couch with yesterday's newspaper in his lap. Jordan saw that he had finished only about a quarter of the crossword puzzle that his dad started at breakfast.

"Tough one, huh?" Jordan asked.

"Yeah. I guess my mind isn't up to it today. How was school?"

"It was good. I have some nice teachers. I got compliments on the drawing I did in art class. And . . ." Jordan paused for effect, "I convinced them to let me change the name of the book club to X-Libris." Jordan pretended that the name change meant nothing to him, but he couldn't hide his excitement. "I didn't think they were going to go for it, but they did. I convinced them to change it!"

His father smiled. "Well, congratulations!" He got up off the couch and patted Jordan on the shoulder.

"Here's today's paper," Jordan said, handing it over. "Maybe it has an easier crossword puzzle." He headed to his room where he unpacked his bookbag and put its contents in their proper places. Once he was done, he settled into his desk chair and opened the padded envelope.

There were a few pieces of junk mail and form letters from the local city councillor. One envelope contained a card addressed to his dad. He still got these on occasion. They were from some of his clients from the vet clinic. They were usually notes hoping that he was doing well and that they would never forget how he had taken care of Rex, or Cleo, or whatever their pet was called. He would give that to his dad to open. It would make him feel good.

Then there was an envelope addressed to his mom. Jordan opened it. It was an invitation to a class reunion. The reply card had a series of check boxes to let them know if you were going: "Can't Wait — I'll be there!"; "I Sure Hope I Can!"; "I'm So Sad, I Can't!" Jordan looked at this and added a fourth: "Deceased — Sorry." He checked this and stuffed the card in the return envelope. He would mail it back tomorrow.

Things that reminded Jordan that his mother wasn't alive made him feel sad, so he focused on the part of her that was still with him: her books. Maybe that was why tomorrow was so important. Tomorrow was when he would try to convince students to sign up for the book club. In the long history of clubs at Playter Heights, the book club (which started long before Jordan was even born) was considered one of the nerdiest. But he wasn't going to let that stop him.

On sign-up day, each club was assigned a table. Jordan planned to put up a display of books on his. He hoped the display would entice people to join. As president of the club, he had decided on the theme. This year it would be science fiction. He looked at the wall of books in his room and selected which of his mother's collection he would take in. He chose the best-known books he had. Then his eyes rested on a small book by Issac Asimov, the writer who came up with the three laws of robotics:

**Law One – A robot may not injure a human being, or, through inaction, allow a human being to come to harm;**

**Law Two – A robot must obey the orders given it by human beings except where such orders would conflict with the First Law;**

**Law Three – A robot must protect its own existence as long as such protection does not conflict with the First or Second Laws.**

That was from *I, Robot* and Jordan found that so cool. The book he selected, however, had been a gift to his mother when she was young. It came in its own cardboard box and was a special edition volume of *Pebble in the Sky*, made more important because it was signed by the author. It had been one of his mother's most prized possessions. Jordan carefully wrapped it in a towel, then another one and placed it in his bookbag.

He finished packing up the books and made his way to the kitchen. He liked to help out around the apartment, and tonight he got to pick what they would have for dinner — frozen pizza. As he took the box out of the freezer, he said to himself, "Today was a good day. Tomorrow is going to be a good day." He repeated this three times. Maybe just saying it over and over would make it true.

# 06 The Same Old School Grind

JORDAN'S ALARM WENT OFF AT SIX. He took his morning shower and dressed in the clothes he'd laid out for himself the night before. He moved to the kitchen and made oatmeal with fresh blueberries and put exactly half a cup of yogurt in a bowl which he placed beside his morning cup of tea. He prepared his father's usual breakfast of toast and coffee and got it set out for him at his place at the table.

Jordan looked at the table. If his mom were

here she would have had a small vase of flowers as a centrepiece. He went into the living room and brought back a small cactus that bore a single bloom. That would have to do.

He checked his watch. There was still time so he decided to make his dad a sandwich for lunch. He left it on a plate in the fridge and called his father. "Breakfast is ready."

The two sat at the table and ate their breakfast. His dad glanced through the paper while Jordan sat quietly. There was little conversation. That had always been his mother's thing. Jordan liked to think the silence was a man's thing, and something he shared with his father.

"So, what's on the calendar for you today?" his dad finally asked.

"It's club sign-up day. Other than that, the same old school grind." That was one of his mother's phrases she'd use when he came home from school. *How'd your day go? Same old school grind?*

His dad smiled and said, "I'll clean up if you want

to head out."

The clock read 7:15.

"Sure. Thanks. Your lunch is in the fridge."

Jordan got up and gave his dad an awkward side hug goodbye, then went to retrieve his bookbag by the front door. From inside he pulled out his paper day-timer and wrote *Pick up paper for Dad* in the 3:00 p.m. time slot. In a school full of kids who kept track of things on their phones, Jordan realized he was different. He always used a paper day-timer. Paper day-timers never died and never needed to be recharged.

Once his note was done he headed out for the fifteen-minute walk to school.

It was early and he knew that the main door of the building would be locked, so he walked around to the back and knocked loudly on a basement window. A few minutes later, Mr. Jenkins opened one of the school's back doors.

"Good morning, Mr. Jenkins,"

"Good morning. Here to help?" the caretaker asked.

"You bet."

Jordan followed Mr. Jenkins into the school and up to the second-floor hallway where several tables were already in place for the club sign-up day. Pieces of paper had been taped along the wall by Mrs. Singleton, the school's secretary, each labelling the position of a club's table. Most of them ran down the long main hallway across from the windows overlooking the courtyard. The table for the book club was situated at the end, in the corner where the hallway turned toward the library. It meant that Jordan didn't have to set up beside any other club. He'd explained to Mrs. Singleton that being that close to any of the more energetic club's members might prevent the more bookish students from approaching his table. In truth, he just felt too nervous to be that close to them. It also meant that Mr. Jenkins could provide him with a larger table without making it look like Jordan was being given special treatment. Many of the students already thought of him as special, and not in a good way.

Another benefit of the longer table was that it gave Jordan space to set up his book display.

"Mr. Jenkins," Jordan said, "Mrs. Singleton forgot the Cheerleader Squad again."

"I'll grab another table."

As soon as Mr. Jenkins left, Jordan pulled down the Bookwormers sign and replaced it with the one which read X-Libris.

# 07 Welcome to Playter Frights

JORDAN ASSEMBLED THE DISPLAY of some of his mother's favourite science-fiction novels and lined up his supply of pens and a sign-up sheet. Other clubs had tablets for people to sign up on. Some of them were also taking new members' photos and printing them on membership cards. A pen and pad of paper were good enough for Jordan. He had little difficulty remembering the faces of the X-Libris membership. All four of them.

It wasn't long before the hallway was full of

students. Lots of them were stopping at the tables, especially those with large computer screens that displayed what the clubs did. Hardly anyone stopped at Jordan's table. He was used to it, being ignored, unless he was being taunted. "Loser," "Freak," "Nerd" — those insults he let roll off him. What he hated were the people who bumped into his table. After each bump, he'd straighten out his pens, realigning them all perfectly, and set his books back in place.

Jordan had just finished fixing his display for the third time when he noticed someone moving quickly down the line of tables, smoothly gliding around the other students. It was the boy who'd been late for homeroom yesterday. Jordan couldn't take his eyes off him. Today Jordan noted what he wore, just in case Emma asked — tight red jeans and a blue t-shirt. The boy kept glancing at the signs on the wall, then at a table, then moving to the next. He looked like he was searching for something specific.

Jordan was amazed at the way he moved, zigzagging through the crowd without bumping into anyone, unlike the first time Jordan had seen him. He looked like he could have been a dancer. If it had been Jordan, he would have rammed into several people, and probably been knocked to the floor for doing so. When the boy had finished checking out the Science Fair table he made his way straight toward Jordan. There was an instant fluttering in Jordan's stomach again.

He reached Jordan's table, read the sign, looked at the table, looked down the remaining library hall, which was empty, and then glanced back from where he had come.

He turned to Jordan and asked, "Where's the table for the Gay-Straight Alliance?"

Jordan felt slightly dizzy. This boy was so . . .

Jordan forced a nervous smile. "Uh . . . They're called Gender and Sexuality Alliances, and we don't have one."

"Huh," the boy said, turning away. As he turned, he bumped the table ever-so slightly, causing Jordan's pens to pivot on the spot and one of his books to slide off its prop.

Jordan placed the book back on its stand and put his pens in order.

The boy spun back around. "Is that even allowed — to *not* have one?"

Jordan shrugged. "You're new here, aren't you? Welcome to Playter Frights."

The boy clamped his lips together until they almost disappeared into his mouth, then he walked back to the Science Fair table, where a single female student in a pristine white lab coat was sitting, playing on her phone. He leaned in and said something to her, then took the unused chair beside her, returning with it to Jordan's partially empty table. He plunked it down behind the table next to Jordan.

"Hope you don't mind. But yours is the only table with space."

Before Jordan could protest, the boy grabbed Jordan's roll of masking tape. Then, with the back of his hand, he shoved all of the pens and pencils toward Jordan.

"Equality requires space," the boy said as he

unrolled a length of tape and divided the table in two. He took one of Jordan's markers and a sheet from Jordan's paper supply — and not one of the small pieces, but the largest size Jordan had — and started to write. "What did you say they were called? The Gay-Straight Alliances?"

Jordan was stunned. All he could do was squeak out, "Gender and Sexuality . . ."

He watched as the boy drew up his own *unapproved* sign, even adding a rainbow which he coloured using highlighters borrowed from the cheerleaders, then taped his sign on the wall behind him.

"You can't just . . . do that!" Jordan sputtered.

"Why not?"

"Because . . . you just *can't*. If everybody just put up their own signs and created their own clubs —"

"That's not going to happen," the boy interrupted. "This place has the school spirit of a prison."

"A place, I'm guessing, you've probably had some experience with," Jordan replied.

The boy smiled. "Wouldn't you like to know?

I'm Nathan, by the way," he said, holding out his hand.

Jordan didn't move.

"And you are . . . You do have a name, don't you, or has this place stripped you of that and just given you a number?" Nathan asked.

"Jordan," he managed to get out.

"Nice to meet you, Jordan. And sorry for barging in like that and taking over. I just can't sit by when I see injustice."

Jordan tried to stay calm as he thought about the number of rules Nathan had broken in such a short period of time. But before he could finish his thought a shadow fell across the table.

"So, you're not only a nerd, but you're a fag now."

Jordan recognized Brody's voice, and his stomach gave a nervous twinge.

"No. *I'm* the fag," Nathan piped up. "Care to sign up for the Gender-Sexuality Alliance? If I read you right, you'd be our first straight member."

Jordan froze. He couldn't breathe or blink. He just waited for Nathan to be punched through the brick wall behind him. He was sure that Brody could do that.

"Freaks!" Brody spat, then shoved the table with both arms, sending the entire book display tumbling onto the floor.

Jordan felt himself starting to unravel. He grabbed the edge of the table and focused on his breathing.

*Not today. Not in front of everyone.*

Brody laughed and turned away.

Time seemed to stand still.

Then Nathan leapt over the table yelling, "Nothing worse than a jock whose brain is smaller than his tiny dick!"

Brody whirled around, but before he could respond, Mr. Childs, the school librarian, was marching up the hall toward them. "What's going on here?"

Brody just sneered and pointed at Nathan. "I think this student has a bit of an attitude problem, sir."

Nathan didn't reply. He was busy picking up the

books from the floor, carefully brushing them off, and placing them back on the table. He ignored Brody and turned to Jordan. "I think they're all right." He held up the copy of Isaac Asimov's *Pebble in the Sky.* "This one's got a bit of a ding on the corner."

Jordan stared at the book in Nathan's hand. In his mind, the cover was ruined.

"Just a sec," Nathan said. "I think I can fix this." He carefully bent the corner back into position, then took a small piece of tape and reinforced it from the inside.

He handed it back to Jordan. "There. It's almost as good as new."

Mr. Childs interrupted. "The books can wait. Who started this?"

Nathan turned to face him. "I did."

"Would you care to tell me *why?*"

"Perhaps at detention, sir."

Mr. Childs simply looked at Nathan and said, "Three p.m. in the library."

The librarian turned to Brody. "Move along or I'll see you in detention as well."

Brody smirked at Jordan and said, "See ya later, loser," then walked away.

As Mr. Childs went back down the hallway, Emma pushed through the crowd. She formed a barrier between the departing students and Jordan. "Are you all right?" she asked, carefully packing up the books while Jordan sat in his chair.

"Here. Let me help," Nathan added.

"Just leave me alone," Jordan replied. He could feel tears coming.

Nathan said, "I just wanted to help. I told you, I can't stand injustice."

"Please, just leave . . . You have to obey the rules. If you don't . . ." Jordan didn't want to finish the sentence — it was too real for him — but it just came out anyway. "Lives get broken."

"What does that mean?" Nathan asked.

"Just leave me alone," Jordan repeated.

Nathan stared at Jordan and Emma for a moment, then quickly walked away leaving them to pack up the rest of the books.

# 08 Shakespeare Must Die

JORDAN SAT AT MR. JENKINS'S DESK ALONE, eating his cheese sandwich. After the morning he'd had, he needed a space away from everyone. The caretaker had been called away to unplug a sink in the staff lunchroom. Jordan looked through the open doorway to Mr. Jenkins's workroom. On the workbench, tools were scattered everywhere, as well as several jars filled with an assortment of nuts, bolts, and screws. He finished his sandwich but couldn't take his eyes off the tools. He stood up and walked over to them. They were pretty dirty. Then he noticed a pair of work gloves . . .

It didn't take Jordan long to organize all the tools, first by type, then by size. He found sorting the nuts, bolts, and screws a little more time-consuming given the bulky gloves he was wearing, but, with a little effort, he sorted those as well. Organizing Mr. Jenkins's workbench helped to calm him down. As he sorted, he thought of Nathan and all the trouble he'd caused. But Nathan had also stood up to Brody and cared about the books. He was kind of brave and exciting and . . . dangerous. Jordan had to stop thinking about him.

He tucked his bag with the books he had brought for the display in beside the caretaker's desk and wrote a note that said, *I'll be back to pick these up at the end of the day.* He knew they would be safe. As he finished, the school bell rang and Jordan headed to his favourite class — English.

His teacher this year was Miss Street, and she was new. Jordan sat in the first row. He lined up his two pens in the groove at the top of his desk, then cracked open a new notebook. He found himself annoyed that someone had already written "Shakespeare must die!" on his desk.

*A bit late for that*, he thought, taking out his eraser and rubbing out the words.

Jordan glanced toward the door and saw a flurry of coat and backpack blowing in from the hall. It was Nathan who plunked himself at the desk next to him, a desk Jordan had hoped would be occupied by Emma.

Nathan's face was beaming as he said, "Here we are again. Isn't this great?"

"Yeah. Great . . ." Jordan said. He saw Emma enter the room. She smiled at him and took the last available desk which was at the back of the class.

"Good afternoon, everyone. I'm Miss Street. Welcome to English class. First, I'd like to tell you what you'll be facing in your reading list. This semester it will include Albert Camus's *The Plague*, appropriate, given the pandemic we've all just been through; *Cry the Beloved Country* by Alan Paton; *The Marrow*

*Thieves*, by Cherie Dimaline; Margaret Atwood's *The Handmaid's Tale* — and don't think because you can watch the TV series that you don't have to read the book; and finally, yes, the one you all love to hate — William Shakespeare."

There was a collective groan throughout the room.

"This year it will be his romantic comedy, *Twelfth Night*. Now before you complain about Shakespeare's relevance today, I'd like to remind you that his works introduced over 1,700 new words he created that are still widely used today. Words like: obscene, alligator, bedroom, and gossip; an interesting combination of words if you worked them into a single sentence."

There were a few laughs as students came up with their own sentences involving gossips talking about obscene alligators in the bedroom.

*Childish*, Jordan thought.

Miss Street continued. "And remember, if it weren't for *Romeo and Juliet* there would be no *West Side Story*. And *The Lion King*? That's *Hamlet*."

Nathan shot up his hand.

"Yes?" Miss Street asked.

"Won't we be studying any gay writers, like Oscar Wilde?"

Jordan's stomach twisted into a knot. *Why is he doing this and why is everyone looking in our direction?*

Miss Street replied, "Not specifically, but if you want to read an extra book and write a report on it, I would be happy to consider giving you extra credit for it."

Nathan smiled.

"Now, this year we'll be trying something different. All the English classes will be doing team presentations based on their Shakespeare studies. These presentations will be done in front of the whole school at the end of the semester."

Nathan's hand shot up again.

"Yes?" Miss Street asked.

"Can we pick our own teams?" he said, looking at Jordan.

"Your team can include anyone in class, but the

presentation must involve the book we're studying this year. Or you can try and find a modern story based on Shakespeare's *Twelfth Night*. The results of your team's presentation will make up twenty-five percent of your mark for the term."

"Partners?" Nathan asked, still looking at Jordan.

"Sure," Jordan said before he realized his mouth was moving.

*What have I done?*

Jordan looked back toward Emma for support. Emma just smiled and gave him a little wave.

He spent the rest of the class staring out the window, trying to ignore the tightness in his chest.

# 09 Four Things He Could Smell

AS SOON AS THE BELL RANG, Jordan bolted for the door. He ran down to Mr. Jenkins's office and retrieved his bookbag. He left the school as quickly as he could and ran until he was away from where any of the other students would see him.

Everything that had happened today hit him all at once. He was having a hard time catching his breath. He knew he needed to get home quickly. Jordan didn't want anyone to see him like this — heading into full panic attack mode.

*Why can't I be stronger?*

On a quiet street, he took a deep breath in through his nose, then slowly released it out through his mouth, just like his therapist had taught him.

*I've had these before*, he acknowledged. *It's just my brain short-circuiting. I have to refocus my thoughts.*

He closed his eyes and identified four things he could smell: fresh-baked bread, the exhaust of the cars on the street, the dog poo that someone hadn't picked up, the cigarette smoke from the guy walking by.

He took time identifying each one, and he began to feel a bit calmer.

Next, Jordan opened his eyes and looked for four things that he could touch. He reached for each one and described them in his mind: the rough surface of the wooden streetlight post, the sharp edges of the bakery's brick wall, the heat of the metal bus stop pole, the soft sides of his leather bookbag.

Jordan slowed his breathing and gave himself a task. He continued to the corner store where he picked up his dad's newspaper then made his way home.

Once he was safely in his building, he forced himself to walk up the stairs, through the door of his apartment, and straight to his bedroom.

Jordan dropped his bookbag and newspaper on his desk and threw himself on his bed, burying his face in his pillow. He started to sob. In a few minutes, there was a gentle tap on his door. He heard his father's voice.

"Jordie?" he said softly.

Jordan heard his father enter the room and felt him sit on the edge of the bed. He said nothing else, but put his hand on Jordan's shoulder, then moved to his back and gently rubbed it in small circles. Jordan focused on his father's hand, picturing it as if he was watching from above.

"Bad day at school, kiddo?" his father eventually asked.

"I'd rather not talk about it," Jordan said. After a minute he added in a whisper, "I'm so sorry."

"For what?"

"For being such a freak."

"You are not a freak," said his father. "Never say that. You've just been through a lot over the last two years. We both have." He continued to gently rub Jordan's back just like his mother used to do. A few moments later he asked, "Are you going to be okay?"

Jordan nodded. "I brought you your paper," he said, pointing to his desk.

His dad smiled. "You remembered even though you were having a bad day. Tell you what, why don't you stay here and I'll fix us some supper." He patted Jordan on the shoulder again then left the room.

In no time his dad was back with scrambled eggs and toast. He brought it to Jordan on a tray that had fold-down legs. "There. Breakfast for dinner. *Bon appetit.* I'll let you eat in peace," he said, then left the room, closing the door behind him.

# 10 Dr. Frankenstein

AFTER JORDAN FINISHED HIS DINNER, he looked at the bookbag on his desk and decided he couldn't delay any longer.

He unpacked the books and checked each one, looking for damage. He dusted each book off and put them back on the shelf in their correct place. The last book he looked at was the one signed by Isaac Asimov. That morning he'd thought twice about bringing it in, then a third time *(It'll be all right)* before putting it in his bookbag. Now it had a bent corner . . . Wait a minute. He looked at each of the corners, and they all appeared to be normal. Then he remembered the kindness that Nathan had shown him. He opened the cover and saw the small piece of tape.

In his mind, he heard Nathan say, "*There. It's almost as good as new.*"

*Nathan* . . . Butterflies swirled in Jordan's stomach.

He looked carefully at the book. It *did* look almost as good as new. Jordan held the book tightly. If broken books could be healed, why couldn't he? He just had to bend his own twisted corners back into shape.

He needed to prove to himself that he could change his habits and he didn't always need to be in control.

Jordan made a decision.

He stood in front of one of the shelves lining the walls and carefully removed all of the books, piling them on his bed and floor. Then he closed his eyes, picked one up and put it on a shelf. Then another, and another until, in time, all of the books had been randomly placed, without regard to subject, author, title or even colour or height of the cover.

He looked at his work. There was something refreshing about the chaos. He felt like Dr. Frankenstein. He had taken all of these individual parts and created something new. And it was *alive!*

He stared at the bookcase. Where *did* that book that Nathan fixed go? *Oh my god . . .* Where was *any* book? In his excitement to break with the "old Jordan," he'd even put some books back with their titles toward the wall. What had he done? Jordan had taken his perfectly calm and ordered world and, like Dr. Frankenstein, had created a monster that was going to eat him alive.

It took Jordan several hours to re-sort his library. It was eleven o'clock when he crawled into bed and thought about the past two days.

"Focus on the positive." *What good things happened? No books were destroyed. Brody didn't punch me (that's not really a positive. That's a negative, with a spin). Okay — And I got the name change for the book club approved!*

Then there was Nathan. *He's disruptive. He brings chaos. But he fixed my book. And he's cute . . . and gay. Can I trust him? I'm not sure . . . I need to take control.*

Then Jordan had an idea — an idea that would take care of more than one of his problems. He would have to wait until next week's book club meeting to put his plan into action.

He thought about what he would say and ran it over and over again in his mind. It was a long time before he finally fell into a restless sleep.

# 11 X-Libris

JORDAN HAD TROUBLE FOCUSING on his classes. Today was the first meeting of the book club and he wondered if anyone new would show up. Nobody had signed up the previous week, but maybe someone would come because they'd seen the table.

The day dragged on. The only excitement was an explosion in the chemistry lab which had filled the school hallways with a smell like a couple of warring skunks.

When the bell rang at the end of his final class, Jordan headed off to the library, and walked up to Mr. Childs's desk.

"Mr. Childs, I need the key for Activities Room A, please."

"What for?"

"The book club?"

"Bookwormers, isn't it?"

Jordan sighed. "Its new name is X-Libris."

The librarian didn't look impressed as he slid a book over to Jordan. "Sign out the key here."

Jordan signed and dated the register, writing the new club name in the last column.

As president of the club (there had been no election for the position because no one else wanted to do the job) Jordan had been given access to supplies and photocopying. His only responsibility was to set up the room for club meetings and clean up afterward. He also had to file a year-end report, a job that was normally handled by the club secretary, but that was him as well because, again, no one else volunteered to do it. Jordan had printed and laminated a new sign: **X-Libris. Here, we set the words free.** He taped it to the door of the room.

Emma was the first to show up, followed by Yan and Jinx. Jordan could never remember Jinx's real name. He had been in the book club since last year and it was too embarrassing to ask his name now. So, Jinx it was, although Jordan thought his first name might be Bob or Joe or . . . well, Jinx it would stay.

Jordan waited to see if anyone else would arrive and when it was clear that it was just the four of them, he began. "Now that we're all here, I'd like to welcome you to the first meeting of —" but before he could continue a voice interrupted.

"Am I late? I had no idea where to go."

"Nathan! Grab a seat," Emma said. "I hope nobody minds that I invited him."

"What are you doing?" Jordan whispered to her.

She smiled and said, "Just making a new student feel at home." She turned to the others. "Everybody, this is Nathan. I'm sorry, I don't know your last name."

"It's Tremblay. I moved here from Montreal this

summer. My dad's French, but I'm kinda crap at the language so don't expect any help with it from me."

Yan laughed. "I'm Yan Lee."

"Tom Jackson, but people call me Jinx," Jinx said.

*Tom! That was it. How could I have forgotten that?* Jordan thought.

"And I'm Emma Watkins, and this is Jordan Shepherd, who you've already met."

"Of course," Nathan said, smiling at Jordan.

Jordan felt Emma's hand on his right knee. He saw that it was vibrating nervously. *Stop it,* he thought. *You're like a five-year-old who has to pee!* He willed his leg to stay still.

"Okay," Jordan began again after referring to his notes, "as *most* of you know, the school demands that we appoint a secretary. I usually do it, but the school says that we have to give everyone a chance. And, just a reminder, this won't count toward your mandatory volunteer hours. So do we have any members who would like to take on the boringly unglamorous position of secretary of X-Libris?"

"I thought this was Bookwormers?" Jinx said.

"Old news, Jinx. Didn't you see the sign on the door?" Emma asked.

"Oh. That'll take some getting used to," Jinx mumbled.

Yan said, "I like that name. It makes the club sound important."

Nathan said, "I think it's an excellent name, and I'll be happy to record it in the meeting minutes if you'll have me as the club's secretary."

Jordan looked around and before he could say anything else Emma said, "All in favour, raise your hand."

Emma, Yan, Jinx, and Nathan all raised their hands. Emma said, "Well, I guess that settles it."

And, just like that, Nathan had taken something away from Jordan, and it didn't feel good. He felt the tightness in his chest beginning.

*I need to take control.*

Jordan straightened himself in his chair. He had to look like a figure of authority. He took a deep breath and started talking. "We are all in Miss Street's English class, so I don't have to tell you about the insane idea that the English Department has come up with — the presentation of our *Twelfth Night* projects to the school. Nathan asked me if I would be his partner in this craziness and I agreed."

Jordan looked around the room to see if there was any reaction to this news. Strangely there was none.

He continued, "Last week I was thinking about the project and the first thing I thought of was the saying 'There is safety in numbers.' That's when it came to me: why don't we include everyone in X-Libris in the team!"

Jordan nervously waited for the group's response.

"Why not?" Yan said.

"That's a great idea," Emma added.

Jinx just stared at Emma. "I agree with Emma."

"Now, here's what I was thinking," Jordan went on. "Miss Street said we could use something based on *Twelfth Night*. A few years ago, I wrote a story called *The Swordsman's Destiny*. It was adapted from some of the characters and the plot of *Twelfth Night*. Why don't we use that? Almost everyone else will be presenting on the original play. We'd be doing something completely new and different."

Jordan felt energized now that he was back in control of things.

Yan was the first to speak. "So how is this going to work?"

Jordan replied, "I've already written the story. We just have to split it up and each take turns reading it out loud."

Jinx nodded.

Emma said, "I think that's a great idea. All in favour, raise your hands."

Everyone raised their hands . . . except for Nathan, who had a hurt look on his face.

"Motion carried," Emma said.

After everyone had put down their hands Jordan suggested, "Since this *is* a book club, we should decide what we'll be reading this year."

"I think it should be comic books," Jinx said. "Or

what about graphic novels or manga? *Blue Flag!* That would be a good one. It's about a teenage boy and girl who fall in love," he said, looking over at Emma.

Everyone had a different idea of what they should read and before they knew it, half an hour had gone by without any decisions being made and Jordan brought the meeting to a close.

After everyone had left, Jordan started to reset the furniture in the room. He noticed Nathan standing by the door.

"Why did you do that?" Nathan asked.

"Do what?"

"I thought we were going to work on the English presentation by ourselves," Nathan said. "And if I hadn't shown up today, were you going to tell me about this later after everyone else had agreed to work on it?"

Jordan felt the blood rush to his face. "I didn't mean to hurt your feelings. I just needed to take control. And I still want you to be part of the project."

"I'll have to think about it," Nathan said, then walked out.

# 12 The Great Library Sit-In

JORDAN WAS NERVOUS ABOUT SEEING Nathan the next day at school, but he needn't have worried. Nathan wasn't there the next day, or the rest of the week. Jordan didn't see Nathan until the following Wednesday when he mysteriously showed up in English.

"Hey," Jordan said sheepishly.

"Hey," Nathan replied.

"Where were you last week?"

"Did you miss me?" Nathan asked with a wink.

Jordan felt his cheeks getting warm. "Maybe. So where have you been?"

Nathan stared out the window "I was busy . . . with family stuff."

Jordan rearranged the pens on his desk. "Look, I'm sorry about last week. I talked to Miss Street and she approved our project for the presentation . . . if you still want to be a part of it."

Nathan didn't respond immediately then said, "I'm not sure. I was thinking of partnering with one of the jocks."

"What? You'll end up doing all of the work yourself!"

Nathan smirked. "Jordan, I'm only joking."

Jordan sighed. "Oh, thank god. I thought you'd lost it. So, will you be at the X-Libris meeting today?"

"Of course I will," Nathan said. "I'm the secretary."

Jordan paused. "Can I ask you a question?"

"Sure."

"Why did you join X-Libris?"

"Maybe because I think you're . . . interesting. Or maybe it's because I love to read. I get it from my folks. My mom reads all the time, and my dad teaches literature at the University of Montreal. I read a lot of political stuff about gay rights. You know, to learn how to protect myself, but what I really love is poetry."

Jordan looked at him, curious. "Poetry? Like what?"

Nathan leaned toward Jordan, stared directly into his eyes and said,

> "When we do part,
>
> I wish my form would cleave in two,
>
> Each as diff'rent as sun and moon.
>
> One part body, in all its due,
>
> The other, purest soul."

Nathan finished with a slight smile.

Jordan couldn't breathe. He found himself unable to speak.

Nathan held his position for a moment longer, then leaned back. "I find poetry . . . pure. Nothing is wasted. It relaxes me. *You* must read a lot."

Jordan forced himself to take a deep breath and focus. "Yeah . . . We all do. In the club. Well, Emma does. So does Yan, but he's fussier. And Jinx . . . I have no idea why he shows up. I don't think he ever reads."

"Oh, he's got it bad for Emma," Nathan said as if it was the most obvious thing in the world.

"What?"

"Don't you see the way he looks at her? He couldn't keep his eyes off her for a second at the last club meeting."

"But . . . Emma?"

"Well, he's certainly not there for the books."

"I hope you two are discussing your team project." a voice said.

They turned to see Miss Street standing over them.

"We were discussing books, poetry, and the nature of love," Nathan answered.

"As it relates to *Twelfth Night*," Jordan added quickly.

"Good," she said. "I look forward to finding out more about the specifics of your proposal." Then she walked away.

★★★

At the end of class, Yan and Jinx said they were going to the corner store to pick up snacks. Emma, Jordan, and Nathan said they would meet them in Activity Room A, and they made their way to the library.

When they arrived, Jordan walked up to the loans counter where Mr. Childs was working.

"Mr. Childs, we need the key to Activities Room A, please. We have our meeting of X-Libris."

"X . . . ?" The librarian looked at Jordan like he'd spoken to him in Klingon.

"X-Libris . . . The book club."

"Oh. Bookwormers. Why didn't you say so?"

Jordan sighed. *They never listen.*

Mr. Childs stood and went to the big book on his side table and flipped through it. "That's strange. The room is booked for another group."

"But we meet every Wednesday. Every week." Jordan said.

Mr. Childs looked at the book again. "I'm afraid you don't have it booked for today. Someone else has it."

"What?" Jordan yelled.

"Mr. Shepherd, I never thought I'd have to remind *you* of the 'quiet' rule in a library," he said in a loud whisper.

"Who booked it?" Emma asked.

Mr. Childs looked at the register again and pulled out a note. "Ah, I see what's happened. It was re-booked by Mr. Banks. The note here says that it was approved by the principal. Since they're a larger group in need of space, it appears that you have been bumped."

"By who?" Nathan demanded.

Just then Brody walked in, followed by the entire football team.

"Excuse me," Brody said, pushing past Jordan and Emma. "I'd like the key to Activities Room A please, Mr. Childs."

"What?" Jordan squeaked.

Brody looked at him with a sneer on his face. "Football team yoga. Sorry, but the gyms are booked and Room A is the only space big enough to hold us all."

Brody signed the book and took the key from Mr. Childs. "Thank you, sir," he said, then sneered again at Jordan and walked off, followed by a troop of his oversized teammates. Jordan heard one of the players mutter, "Tough luck . . . losers."

Jordan stood there, silent, as Nathan asked, "We'll get it back next week, won't we?"

"I'm afraid not," Mr. Childs answered. "It seems to be booked for the rest of the year."

Jordan couldn't believe what he was hearing. He started taking deep breaths. Emma put her arm around him.

"Are there any other times or spaces available?" Nathan asked, firmly.

"No. We are booked solid."

Nathan pushed himself right up against the counter. "You can't let this happen, Mr. Childs. It is a gross violation of our rights!"

Mr. Childs shrugged his shoulders. "It would appear the needs of the many, that being the football team, outweigh the needs of the few, being you three."

"There are five of us now," Jordan offered up meekly.

"Five, then," Mr. Childs said, "and twenty of them. Now, unless you're on the football team, or in the radio club which is meeting in Room B, I suggest you move along."

"Well, I won't accept this," Nathan said, loudly. "When the rights of the few are trampled into the dust, the rights of the many are sure to follow!" He then sat down on the floor.

Jordan froze.

"What are you doing, young man?" Mr. Childs demanded, as he leaned over and peered at Nathan, who was now far shorter than Mr. Child's desk.

"This is a sit-in!" Nathan called up to him.

"Well, good luck. You're far too small to stop anyone," the librarian said.

"You want me to take up more space? Fine!" Nathan climbed up and sat on the loans counter beside Mr. Childs's desk. He spread his arms out to occupy as much space as he could. "I vow to sit here until this injustice is rectified."

Jordan felt as though he was about to faint. His heart pounded so hard he could feel it in his ears.

Mr. Childs stared at Nathan. "I'm not saying what happened is fair, but if the principal authorized it, there's nothing I can do, no matter how long you sit up there."

"Please," Jordan squeaked out as he tugged on Nathan's pant leg. "Please come down."

Nathan hopped off the counter.

"Let's just go," Jordan whispered.

Nathan turned to Mr. Childs and said, "Libraries are the one place where words are supposed to thrive, but I guess that's not true at *this* school."

Jordan felt Emma gently pulling on his arm, and the next thing he knew, the three of them were heading out the door.

# 13 The Secret Room

JORDAN, EMMA, AND NATHAN sat in the hallway outside of the library, their backs against the lockers.

"I can't believe we have a radio club," Emma said.

"Or that it has more members than we do," Nathan added.

They were soon joined by Yan. "What are you guys doing out here?"

Before Jordan could answer, Jinx arrived with a large bag of chips in his hands, looked around and said, "Nice hall. Is this where we're meeting now? Hi, Emma." He squeezed in and sat beside her.

Jordan sat with his knees clutched to his chest. He couldn't speak.

"Apparently Brody and the football team have taken over our space for their yoga room," Emma said. "Mr. Childs said they had the full backing of the principal's office and, because they have more members than we do, they get the space."

"We have a yoga team?" Jinx asked.

"It's the football team's yoga practice," Emma said.

"Huh," Jinx replied.

Jordan shifted position and started vibrating his knee. He felt Emma take his hand. She gave it a gentle squeeze, and Jordan's knee settled down.

Nathan said, "There must be some other space in this school that we can use."

Jordan took a deep breath to shake the cobwebs out of his brain, then stood up. "Come on."

"Where are we going?" Emma asked.

"Are we going to find a nicer hallway?" Jinx added.

Jordan went to where he knew he could find safety, and someone who would listen. He led the others to Mr. Jenkins who was at his workbench. He seemed to be tinkering with a fan. Mr. Jenkins turned to find that he had an audience.

"Jordan? Emma? . . . and others . . ."

Emma introduced them. "Mr. Jenkins, this is Nathan, Yan, and that's Jinx."

"Well, hello to you all. Oh, Jordan, I've been meaning to thank you for organizing all my tools. It's much easier to find things. Now, what can I do for you?"

"Mr. Jenkins, we need your help," Jordan said.

He laid out the problem, starting with the encounters with Brody in the coffee shop and the stairwell, then the destruction of his display during club sign-up, ending with the loss of Activity Room A.

"So, you see, Mr. Jenkins, we need to find a space, or our club will die, and there's been a book club at

Playter Heights since clubs first started here. Books are important."

Jordan watched as Mr. Jenkins thought about the problem. One of the reasons Jordan liked Mr. Jenkins so much was that he was logical. He was a problem solver. You had to be in order to be a caretaker.

"Come with me," he said eventually.

He led them through the workroom to his office, then through the office to a door that Jordan had never noticed before. The caretaker took out his large ring of keys and sorted through them, finding a bright silver one that he used to unlock the door. It swung open with a loud creak. Mr. Jenkins reached in and flicked on the light.

Everyone gasped.

It was a large room, its walls all covered in paintings. Some were as small as a book cover, others as large as a big-screen TV. There were pictures of animals, so real they looked like photographs. There were paintings of mountains, and deserts, of trees and old cabins. Jordan looked around. There must have been fifty or sixty of them. And in the corner was an easel. Mr. Jenkins explained that it was the original staff room from the time before the school's big extension was built.

Nathan looked at a painting of a deer. "Mr. Jenkins . . . your name is on this. Did you paint it?"

Mr. Jenkins nodded. "I painted that one in 1992 after travelling to Banff National Park. The one over there," he said pointing to a painting of water shooting out of the earth, "is Old Faithful. That's a geyser in Yellowstone National Park in Wyoming in the States. I did that one in . . . 1998, I think."

"They're all so beautiful," Yan said.

"I'm glad you like them. So, how would you like to hold your meetings here?" Mr. Jenkins asked.

"Could we?" Jordan asked, hardly daring to believe it.

"I could set up a table for you in the middle of the room. And I've got plenty of chairs. What do you say?"

"Yes!" they all hollered.

"It's even nicer than the hallway!" Jinx said.

"Well, I'll have a talk with the principal, but I

can't see that he'd have any problems with it. So, if you can give me a few days to get things arranged, you've got a new home."

★★★

Everyone agreed that they could postpone the meeting of X-Libris. Jinx and Yan left, but the other three had one more thing to do.

Jordan, Nathan, and Emma went up to the library. From the main door, they could see that the football team was just wrapping up their yoga session. Jordan asked if the other two could stand down the hall. This was something he wanted to do alone.

As the team left, Jordan held the main library door open for them. He watched Brody sign the key back in. Jordan thought he looked a little surprised to see him there. Brody walked slowly to the main door. Jordan opened it wide for him and smiled.

"What are you smiling at, shrimp?" the jock snarled.

"Nothing. I just wanted to thank you. Because

you needed the room up here, the school found us a much better place for our club."

"Where's that?"

"Wouldn't you like to know?" Jordan replied, letting the door slowly close on Brody's confused face.

# 14 Everything About You Is Unexpected

JORDAN, EMMA, AND NATHAN left the school smiling. As they reached the edge of the school yard Nathan said, "Jordan, do you mind if I walk with you?"

Jordan looked at Emma. He hoped she would pick up on the mildly panicked look on his face and stick around. Instead, Emma said, "I've got a few things to get on the way home, so I'll leave you two alone."

Jordan stared at her so hard he thought his eyes would fall out of his head. Emma smiled, leaned over, and gave him a hug. She whispered in his ear, "You'll be fine," then walked away.

"Which way do you go?" Nathan asked.

"I probably live in the opposite direction of where you're going."

"Where do you live?"

"East," Jordan replied.

"Me too," Nathan said.

Jordan instinctively began to walk home then thought better of it. He wasn't sure he wanted Nathan to know where his apartment was. It seemed too personal. He decided to let Nathan take the lead.

They walked for a few blocks in silence. Jordan finally spoke. "Thanks for sticking up for me back in the library."

"No problem."

Jordan paused then said, "I also never got to thank you for fixing my book on club sign-up day. It was my mother's and she's not alive anymore so it's special, and I kinda freaked out when it got damaged."

"I'm sorry about your mom."

"It happened a while ago . . ." Jordan's voice trailed off, then he continued, "Anyway, you did an amazing job of fixing her book."

"I just kinda bent the corner back and added a little tape."

Jordan stopped and put his hand on Nathan's arm. "That's not the point. It meant a lot to me."

They both stood still.

Nathan eventually said, "Ah . . . I live right over there."

Jordan saw a small, one-storey house with a front yard that was overrun by wildflowers.

"Nice place," Jordan said.

"Wanna come in?" Nathan asked.

"I . . . really should be going home. My dad worries if I'm late."

"Sure." Nathan smiled. "So, I guess I'll see you around tomorrow. Hopefully, Mr. Jenkins gets the okay to let us use that room."

"Yeah," Jordan answered.

"Well, I guess I should get going."

"Yeah, me too."

Neither of them moved.

"You asked me why I joined X-Libris," Nathan said after another moment passed. "It's because of you. Everything about you is . . . unexpected. And I like that."

Jordan didn't know what to say.

Nathan gave him a quick hug, then turned and walked toward his house. He hopped up the stairs and went through the door, closing it behind him.

Jordan stared at the house and tried to catch his breath.

# 15 Four Things He Could Touch

BECAUSE OF THE CAFETERIA'S SMALL SIZE, lunch was served over two half-periods. Jordan was assigned to the first half. As he stepped out of his class, he found Nathan walking beside him. He followed Jordan to his locker. Jordan opened it up and neatly hung his bookbag on the hook. Nathan said, "Mind if I dump mine here? My locker's on the other side of the school."

Without waiting for an answer, Nathan jammed his pack into Jordan's locker and slammed the door shut. Then he invited himself to join Jordan for lunch.

It was pizza day. Not a surprise given that every other day was pizza day, or Peezah Day as Mr. Black, the cafeteria staff monitor, called it.

The lunch lady handed Jordan his pizza. He took the cardboard wheel covered in red sauce and partially melted cheese back to a table in the far corner. He brought his own cutlery with him. He wasn't afraid of catching germs off the school knives and forks. He just couldn't stand using plastic that would be thrown out and sit forever in a dump somewhere. He lined up his knife and fork beside his plate. He placed his glass of milk precisely at the two o'clock position. Meanwhile, Nathan slammed himself down on the bench across from Jordan. He unloaded his tray like he was throwing out garbage. He scooped up his knife and fork and pushed them off to the side, then took a huge bite of his pizza.

"So . . . have you always lived around here?" Nathan asked through his pizza-filled mouth.

"No."

"Me neither. I moved here from Verdun — that's the coolest part of Montreal."

"That's a long ways away," Jordan commented. He pictured Nathan standing on a tree-lined street surrounded by charming old buildings.

"Yeah, hours away, but it feels like a different planet. Toronto's nothing like Montreal. We used to live in an old apartment. Mom called it 'rad.' She does that — uses old-fashioned slang words in public, cuz she knows it drives me *crazy*! Things like 'Daddio' or 'hep cat.' I don't even know what those things mean."

"Daddio is from the fifties," Jordan said, "and is what a woman would call a guy she loved. A hep-cat is a stylish person from the 1940s or fifties who likes jazz music."

Nathan stared at Jordan in surprise.

"I read a lot," Jordan said, with a shrug.

Before he could continue, Jordan saw Brody walk into the cafeteria with one of his jock buddies. He nudged his friend as he pointed to Jordan. Brody walked up to the table.

"So, having lunch with your boyfriend?" he asked Jordan, sneering.

"Oh, we're not boyfriends, but I *am* looking if you're interested," Nathan answered with a smile.

Jordan stared in horror as Brody threw himself at Nathan. Suddenly Nathan became the guy Jordan had seen in the hallway on club sign-up day, gracefully slipping out of the way as Brody hit the table, sending pizza and milk flying everywhere.

Jordan wanted to help, but he couldn't move.

*He's not going to get out of this alive!*

Nathan ran off toward the safety of the lunch lady. Brody ran after him, but was stopped in his tracks by the long, thin arm of Mr. Black. Jordan stared in amazement. Mr. Black had to be a hundred years old. He looked like a skeleton stuffed into a suit.

"Both of you — come with me," he said.

Nathan quickly fell into line as Mr. Black marched him and Brody out of the cafeteria.

Jordan sat in his seat, still not moving a muscle. A young girl who stood nearby looked at him. "You've got a piece of . . ." she said, pointing to his shirt and the large piece of gummy cheese and pepperoni that clung there.

Jordan felt his chest tightening and his pulse start to race. His mind started to short-circuit.

*Everyone's looking at you. They're all looking at the freak.*

Jordan clenched his fists and whispered to himself, "Not in front of everyone. Do something. Give yourself a task. Give yourself a task."

He willed himself to clear up his and Nathan's trays and the remnants of their lunches, and slid them into the steel rack by the serving counter. He asked the lunch lady for a wet cloth which he used to wipe down the table. When he was done, he left the cafeteria. In spite of trying to take control, the signs of a pending panic attack hadn't diminished.

*You should have done something to help him!*

"Come on," he whispered. "You need to do this. Push the fear away."

Jordan headed to the school office.

From behind the closed door of the principal's office, he heard a voice booming out, "What did you think you were doing?" Jordan assumed that was directed toward Brody.

Jordan knocked at the vice principal's open doorway.

She looked up at Jordan. "Yes?"

Jordan began to shake with fear. "I'm here about the fight in the cafeteria."

"And?" The vice principal stared.

"Nathan was only defending me. Brody's been harassing me since before school started. I just thought the principal should know."

"Why don't you tell him yourself?"

Jordan felt his leg beginning to shake, but he had to go through with this. He owed it to Nathan. "I want to do this in a way that doesn't cause more trouble —"

"For you?" she interrupted.

"Yes."

Jordan was now having trouble breathing.

The vice principal said, "You don't look so well."

Jordan found the words he needed. ". . . Panic attack."

She looked at him with concern and said, "Why don't I take you to the nurse's office to calm down. I'll send a note to your afternoon teachers and explain that you won't be in class. And I'll pass on what you said to the principal."

Jordan followed the vice principal to the nurse's office trying to catch his breath.

The nurse said, "Come in Jordan. What's going on?"

"Panic attack."

The nurse looked him up and down. "Have you had one of these attacks before?"

"Yes, but not usually at school. I know what to do." Jordan immediately walked into the inner room, sat on the edge of a chair and said, "I just need space. On my own."

She stared worriedly at him.

"Trust me," he managed to croak out.

"I'll be at my desk," the nurse replied with a nod.

"I'll check in with you shortly. In the meantime, call me if you need anything."

Jordan closed the door. He tried to catch his breath. He felt as though he was choking, gasping for limited air, even though the logical part of his brain told him that he was breathing easily. His hands grasped out in front of him like they were trying to grab a hold of something, anything that he could use to pull himself out of the moment.

"Please, please, please make it stop," he whispered to himself.

His hands started to hammer down on his thighs. They pounded again and again.

He stood up, then sat down. He paced the length and width of the room, gulping in air like the room was going to run out of it, rubbing his knuckles against his legs.

He collapsed back down on the chair and closed his eyes.

*Think of something else. Anything else.* He pictured his mother's face. It calmed him a little. He slowly took a deep breath in through his nose, then gradually released it out through his mouth. Jordan found the strength to begin refocusing his mind. He closed his eyes and identified four things he could smell: the tang of the pizza sauce on his shirt, the sharp odour of antiseptic, the lemony scent of the floor polish, and the rot of a half-eaten apple in the garbage can.

He felt a bit calmer.

Next, he opened his eyes and looked for four things that he could touch. He reached for each one and described them in his mind: the smooth plastic covering of the chair, the warmth of the glass in the window, the coolness of the metal filing cabinet beside him, the softness of the cotton balls in the jar on the counter.

Just as his breathing was calming down there was a knock at the door. Nathan poked his head in.

"Are you all right?" Nathan asked. He reached out and touched Jordan on the shoulder.

Jordan was still shaking. He just nodded.

"The vice principal told me what you did for me.

That was really brave. I got off with a warning. Brody got a week of detention." He entered the room and closed the door. "The vice principal also told me you were here. I wanted to make sure you were okay."

*Thank god he didn't see me a few minutes ago.*

Jordan chose his words carefully. "I'm better now but look at me. I can't leave all covered in food." His voice cracked.

"Here," Nathan said, taking off his sparkling dark blue outer shirt. Underneath he wore a plain white t-shirt. "Put this on."

Jordan took off his pizza-stained top and put on Nathan's shirt. He looked at himself in the mirror.

"It looks a lot better on you than me," Nathan said.

Jordan managed a weak smile.

"Look," Nathan went on, "the vice principal was going to let our teachers know we won't be in class this afternoon. Let's grab our bags and get out of here."

Jordan nodded. He let the nurse know that he was okay, then led Nathan back to his locker. They grabbed their stuff and headed out. Jordan had never left school early other than for a doctor's appointment. He didn't feel right doing it, but he knew there was no real reason to stick around. Just in case, he insisted on leaving by the back door. Today had been bad enough without someone seeing him and accusing him of skipping school.

# 16 Not Not Normal

"I'M SORRY I CAUSED SO MUCH TROUBLE," Nathan said as they walked. "I never meant to. I just . . . I can't stand bullies. Why can't people just treat everyone nicely? Just because someone's different doesn't mean they should be treated like crap."

Before Jordan could stop himself, he said, "What do you mean by different?"

"Well," Nathan said, "I'm gay and you're kind of nervous and always organizing things —"

"You mean I'm a freak."

"No, I said different, and different isn't necessarily a bad thing," Nathan said.

Jordan started to feel anxious. His heart began to race. He was having trouble breathing again as his thoughts started to swirl.

*No!*

"I gotta go," Jordan said. He began to run, crossing the street with his head down. He heard the squeal of brakes and a loud horn as a car came to an abrupt stop, nearly hitting him. Jordan looked up, froze for a moment, then ran into a park on the other side of the road. He had no idea where he was going. He just knew he had to run. Run from everything. He finally slowed down, and then stopped.

He heard footsteps approaching from behind and felt a hand tug on his shoulder. He gasped.

"Hey, it's just me," Nathan said as he turned him around.

Jordan tried to calm himself, but instead of finding things to focus on that would put him in the present moment, all he could think of was all of the trouble Nathan had caused over the last few weeks: taking over his sign-up table; the book display falling; trying to take over his book club; sitting with him at lunch — messy Nathan; the fight; the food all over his best t-shirt that was so clean that morning. Jordan started to shut down. He did the one thing he didn't want to do in front of Nathan: he started to cry.

"Hey. Hey. It's okay. You're okay now. You're safe."

Jordan heard Nathan's voice and felt a hand gently rubbing his back; like his mother used to do when he was upset; like his father had done the other day.

"Come here." Nathan led Jordan to a park bench, under a large oak tree. The bench faced away from the pathway, looking onto a small rose garden. Jordan was so exhausted he had no energy to resist. Nathan helped him take off his bookbag and then sat down beside him, continuing to gently rub Jordan's back in slow circles. He began to calm down. His sobbing stopped. His breathing slowed. Jordan felt the heavy weight just below his rib cage gradually start to disappear.

Nathan looked at him. There was no judgment in his eyes, only concern.

"I'll stay with you until you feel better," Nathan said, "then I'll walk you home if that's where you want to go. I just need to know you'll be okay."

"I don't think I'll ever be okay. I don't think I can."

"Why?"

"Because . . . because I'm not normal."

Nathan said, "You're *not* not normal. You're unique, special, you're . . . interesting."

Jordan replied, "Interesting?"

Nathan smirked. "I mean in a good way. We all have things that make us different, and maybe that's a good thing."

The two sat there for a long time, saying nothing. It was like Nathan knew that silence was what Jordan needed most right now.

He breathed in the scent of the roses from the garden. When he felt in control again Jordan said, "I think I'm ready to go home now. I have to get dinner started. It's my turn today."

"Let me walk with you."

"Okay."

Jordan and Nathan walked first to the store to pick up a newspaper, then to the front door of the Belvedere Apartments.

Jordan said, "Well, this is me."

"If you ever need to talk, you can give me a call," Nathan said, then gave Jordan his number. Jordan added it to the only other two numbers in his phone's contact list.

"And in case I need anything, can I have your number?" Nathan asked.

"Sure," Jordan said, and tapped his number into Nathan's phone.

Nathan hugged Jordan and said, "Take care of yourself," then slowly walked away.

Jordan stared after him, still feeling the echo of Nathan's hug lingering in his shoulders and back.

He made his way up to his apartment and as usual, took his father his paper.

His dad looked up at him. "How was your day?"

Jordan considered telling him the truth and then said, "Same as always."

"Is that a new shirt?"

"I borrowed it from a friend."

His dad smiled. "It's pretty stylin.' Your friend has good taste."

Jordan blushed. "I'm gonna start my homework." He ran to his room and looked in the mirror. The shirt *was* stylin.'

His phone buzzed. It was a text from Emma.

**I heard you got into a fight in the cafeteria.**

He decided to call her instead of texting back.

"Are you okay?" she said as soon as she answered.

"It wasn't me. It was Nathan. He got into a fight with Brody."

"Oh my god — is he still alive?"

"He kinda won, if you can believe it. For now."

"That must have been scary."

"It was. Nathan walked me home. He gave me his number. Emma . . . I think he likes me —"

Emma squealed.

"— and I think I'm falling for him, and it scares me."

"I told you this was going to be your year," Emma said triumphantly.

"I gotta go make dinner. And, Emma — don't say anything about this to anyone. I don't want to mess this up."

"I promise. Okay, bye. See you tomorrow."

As Jordan disconnected, he smiled. He knew it was a promise she would keep.

# 17 An Umbrella-Sort-of-Day

"I'M OFF TO SCHOOL, DAD. Your lunch is in the fridge. I made sweet pepper slices this time."

"Thank you, Jordie. Have a great day."

"You too, Dad."

Jordan left the apartment and rode the elevator down to the lobby. When the door opened, there, chatting up a storm with Mr. Swan, was Nathan.

"Oh, gotta go. My friend's here," Nathan said. "Have a great birthday, Mr. Swan."

Jordan was bothered by two things. First, that he had wanted to wish Mr. Swan a happy birthday, but now it would look like he'd only remembered it was his birthday because he'd heard Nathan say it; and second — what was Nathan doing in his lobby?

"Good morning, Jordan!" Nathan said, smiling.

"I found your friend sitting on the front steps, so I brought him in out of the rain," Mr. Swan said.

Jordan hadn't even looked at the weather. He wasn't prepared for rain. He peered out of the front door, trying to decide if it was an umbrella-kind-of-rain or a full-raincoat-downpour.

"I think you'll find it's an umbrella-sort-of-day," Mr. Swan said, as if he had read Jordan's mind. He pulled out two umbrellas from behind the desk and handed them to the boys.

"Thank you, Mr. Swan," Nathan said. "I'll bring it back right after school."

Jordan wasn't sure if he liked Nathan being so friendly with Mr. Swan. He didn't have many people in his life he could talk to, so he was careful about sharing them. And now he found he was also sharing the apartment's supply of umbrellas with Nathan. Then he felt guilty for being so selfish when it came to sharing things and people with the boy who had come to his rescue yesterday.

*Tell him how you really feel . . .*

The butterflies fluttered madly inside his stomach. Jordan breathed in through his nose, out through his mouth, calmed himself, and led Nathan out into the rain.

"I'm sorry to just show up like this," Nathan said, "but my mother had a call from the principal last night about what happened. She wanted to walk me to school this morning in case Brody tried to get revenge."

"Oh no! Does she want to mark you for life?"

"Exactly! So, I told her I was going to walk to school with you, and if anything happened, you'd be there to help."

"What did you tell her I was going to do? Distract him by passing out?"

They both laughed. Nathan brushed his hand

against Jordan's. Jordan inhaled sharply. He wondered if Nathan had done that on purpose.

"She wasn't after details. Just an overall idea of a plan." Nathan smiled at Jordan and rested his hand on his shoulder.

Jordan stopped. "Oh no. I forgot to bring your shirt that I borrowed. I had it all ready this morning. It's sitting on my bed."

"Don't worry about it. Keep it. It looks better on you anyway."

Jordan smiled, his cheeks warming. "Thanks . . . So, what did your dad say about the fight?"

"Nothing. My mom and dad are divorced. That's why we moved here, to start over again in a new place." Nathan stared down at the pavement as they walked. "I know it really hurt my mother when he left. She always pretended things were okay, but I could tell. I think she thought the hurt would stay in Montreal, like it was somehow anchored there, like one of those ghosts that can't leave the house they died in."

"My dad did the same thing when my mom

died," Jordan said. "He just walked away from our old life like it would make him feel less . . . sad."

Nathan nodded. "I miss my dad, although Mom says we're better off without him."

"Why did he leave?"

"Because I came out. I was thirteen."

"Coming out at thirteen must have been scary," Jordan said.

"My mom was great about it. She was one hundred percent behind me. It was almost like she was the one who came out, not me." Nathan fell silent.

Jordan hesitated. "And your dad?"

Nathan walked in silence for a bit longer before speaking. "It wasn't so good with him. He didn't accept it. At all. He blamed Mom for babying me and said that all I needed was some manly influences to make me less queer-acting. Mom laughed because Dad wasn't exactly . . . overly butch. Anyway, they split up later that year . . . and it was because of me."

"Is that what he told you?" Jordan asked.

"No. It's just what I feel." Nathan paused. "You

know, I think you'd like my mom if you met her. She's like you. She loves to read. My mom's doing it all the time. Books on self-healing, mostly. She says she's a real hippy, like the flower children from the sixties. But she's not that old. God, can you imagine having a mother that old? I'd like you to come over and meet her sometime."

Nathan seemed excited by the possibility of Jordan coming over, but Jordan wasn't too sure he wanted to go. What if he started to have one of his meltdowns there? Or worse — what if he had to go to the bathroom? He hated using someone else's bathroom. It would be so embarrassing if he left a smell.

Jordan's thoughts were interrupted as they rounded the corner a block from the school. Brody and two of his friends were standing there, talking.

Brody stared them down. Jordan froze in place. Nathan took a few steps before turning around and looking at Jordan. He felt the fingers of his right hand nervously tapping on the handle of his umbrella. Nathan came back for him.

"It's okay," he said softly. "He won't do anything. He's just trying to scare us. Just walk with me and pay attention to what I say. Brody doesn't exist. Understand? He's just a big stupid dream."

Jordan nodded, and the two of them walked ahead.

"So, like I said, let's go to my place after school."

"Okay," Jordan said, hesitantly as they started to pass Brody. He purposely looked at Nathan, ignoring Brody's eyes.

Jordan heard Brody say to his friends, "Thanks to them I got detention."

Nathan ignored them and rambled on, "I've got a wicked video setup my dad sent me. Sometimes it pays to come from a divorce."

They stepped onto the walkway that led to the school entrance and continued walking.

"I think we made it," Nathan said.

"Did you hear what he said?"

"I don't think even Brody is stupid enough to try something after yesterday."

Jordan could feel his heart pounding in his chest. He had been certain that they were going to be beaten up. The thought terrified him. He knew he wouldn't be able to do anything to stop it. How could he control a runaway locomotive like Brody?

He heard footsteps coming up the sidewalk behind them. In seconds a hand clamped on Jordan's shoulder. He knew he wasn't going to make it to the school door. The hand pulled back on his shoulder, spinning him around.

"Why are you two walking so quickly? You know how much I hate running."

It was Emma. Nathan broke out laughing. Emma just looked confused.

# 18 Running from Things

JORDAN LOOKED FOR NATHAN at lunch but he was nowhere to be seen, not until the end of the day in English, the last class of the week.

Nathan came in after Jordan and plopped himself into his seat. He looked distracted.

"Okay, class. Settle down," Miss Street said. "Today I'm going to talk about the world as it was when Shakespeare wrote *Twelfth Night*."

She turned to the whiteboard and started to jot

down specific points as she talked.

"*Twelfth Night*, also titled *What you Will*, was written between 1601 and 1602 . . ." she droned on.

Jordan leaned toward Nathan and whispered, "You okay?"

Nathan waited for a moment before he answered. "Just my dad causing trouble for us."

Jordan frowned. "Is there anything I can do?"

Nathan smiled weakly. "I'll be fine."

Miss Street talked for nearly the whole class about the world Shakespeare lived in, what was happening in his life at the time, his writings, and the plagues he had lived through — *enough of the plague already,* Jordan thought.

At the end of the class, Miss Street said, "I'd like you all to spend some time this weekend writing two hundred and fifty words on what it was like for you to live through the COVID-19 plague. I'd like you to present the fruits of your labour in class next week."

"We have to present it to the class?" Jordan whispered.

Nathan said, "Yeah."

"I can't," Jordan replied, feeling his stomach tighten at the thought.

"It's no big deal."

"It is for me," Jordan said. "I don't . . . I can't present in front of a bunch of people. Talking in front of people terrifies me."

"You managed to put up a table for club sign-up day and you're able to talk in front of Emma, me, Yan, and Jinx."

"That's completely different and you know it," Jordan shot back.

"Well, what about *The Swordsman's Destiny*? We'll be presenting on that!"

"But . . . I thought my contribution to that would be . . . I wrote the story, and you guys would do the presenting," Jordan said.

Nathan scowled and snapped his head toward Jordan. "Well, you're gonna have to present in front of people sometime. You can't spend your whole life running from things."

Jordan gripped the edge of his desk. "What if I have a panic attack? What if I puke?"

"The only way you'll find out is if you at least try," Nathan said.

"It's not that easy for me," Jordan replied. "I have problems. You know that."

"You're not the only one with problems, Jordan." Nathan sounded annoyed. "I'm going through a lot too and I'm just trying to push through as best as I can."

Now it was Jordan's turn to get angry. "You've got problems? What have you got to worry about? Your parents' divorce? Lots of people get divorced. It's a better way to end a marriage than your mom dying. My mom's never coming back, and I can't just push through that!"

Jordan grabbed his books and ran out of the classroom.

He didn't stop until he got home.

# 19 An Apology and an Explanation

WHEN JORDAN OPENED THE DOOR to the apartment his father called out, "Did you pick up today's paper? Apparently, there's a great article on rabies in coyotes that live in the valley."

Jordan hadn't picked up his dad's paper. This was important. It was part of their ritual and he had forgotten. "Stupid, stupid, stupid," he scolded himself.

"I'm sorry, Dad. I forgot."

"Don't worry about it. I'll pop out and get it. The

walk'll do me good."

"No. It's my job," Jordan yelled back. "I'll go!"

"Okay," his dad said.

All the way to the corner store Jordan beat himself up over forgetting about his dad. If Nathan hadn't pushed him so hard, he wouldn't have let his dad down like that. The Shop 'n' Bag was out of papers, as was Gwen's Variety and Tom's Milk. He had to go all the way down to the big grocery store south of Danforth Avenue to find one.

*This is what happens when you get involved with someone like Nathan.*

When he got back, the evening doorman was on duty. "You're late today," he said.

"I've already been home," Jordan said, waiting for the elevator. "But I'm stupid and forgot something."

"Happens to the best of us, my friend."

Jordan barged through the apartment door and gave his dad the paper.

"Thanks, kiddo," his dad said. "Best son, ever."

*Not a hard thing to say when I'm the only one you've got.*

“I’ll call you when dinner’s ready,” his dad said as Jordan headed off to his bedroom.

“I’m not hungry!” he shouted back, closing the door a little harder than he meant to.

Jordan wasn’t sure who he was madder at: himself for forgetting the paper, or Nathan for being such a jerk and making him so upset. Before Nathan, everything was in order. Newspapers were always picked up. Books were always put in the right place on the shelf. When things got out of order, when routines were broken, important stuff got missed. Like doctor’s appointments, and . . .

Jordan’s phone chirped with an incoming text. He ignored it. “If he thinks I’m going to talk to him . . .” he muttered to himself before tossing his phone aside and throwing himself onto the bed.

He kept replaying the fight with Nathan over and over in his head. “. . . You can’t spend your whole life running from things.”

*If I’m going to be running from things, it’ll be you!*

Jordan heard the sound of another incoming text.

"No!" he yelled at the phone.

*He thinks he's so much worse off than me. At least his parents are both still alive, even if his dad does live in Montreal. His dad sounds like a jerk anyway and Nathan's probably better off without him.*

A third incoming text chirped. "Go away!" he yelled into his pillow.

Then he realized the texts might be from Emma. He got up and checked his phone. Three texts. All from Nathan. The text previews said:

Please forgive me. I need to explain . . .

And,

I'm so sorry.

The third text was simply an emoji,

Jordan refused to open any of them. "You had your chance, and you blew it."

His phone rang. It was Emma.

"Hey. I waited for you at your locker after school and you never showed up. Are you okay?"

"Can I call you back? I'm just working on something."

"Yeah. Sure," she said, sounding like she didn't believe him.

Jordan disconnected and plopped himself back on the bed. The phone rang again and he answered, "I said I'm kinda busy right now."

For a moment there was silence on the other end.

"I'm so sorry, I just . . . I owe you a huge apology and an explanation."

It was Nathan.

Jordan held the phone to his chest. He took a deep breath, then held the phone back up to his ear and said, "Go on."

"There's no excuse for the way I acted in class."

"No, there isn't."

"But please let me explain before you hang up on me."

The sound of his voice sent the tiniest of shudders through Jordan's body. He waited a few seconds before he said, "Okay."

"My mom called at lunch. I had to go home. We found out that my dad's getting remarried. It's kinda weird, but I know he and Mom weren't going to get back together again. I don't even think I wanted that to happen, but to actually hear that he's moving on without my mom, or me . . . it really hurts."

Jordan could hear Nathan crying.

"My mom didn't handle the news very well. She lost it. She started to throw things at the wall. I was really scared. I didn't know what to do to help her, so I just hid in my room until I could get out of the house and come back to school. I didn't want to say anything. I wasn't sure I could control myself if I started to tell you. And then I said all those horrible things to you . . . I am so sorry. Do you think there's any way you can forgive me?"

"You really hurt me," Jordan said.

"I know."

Jordan took another deep breath to calm himself and steady his voice, and then said, "You had a horrible thing happen to you, and I understand."

"Do you?"

"Yeah. I do. But I need some time to cool down."

"Whatever you want. Just please don't throw me

out of your life."

"How about you meet me at my place Monday morning at 7:30 and we can walk to school together."

"I'd like that."

"Okay. Bye." Jordan disconnected.

There was a knock at the door and his dad poked his head in. "Can I come in?"

Jordan nodded.

"I'm guessing you had a pretty bad day today."

"I've had better," Jordan said, trying to keep his voice calm.

"You know you can tell me anything."

Jordan shrugged. "Yeah, I know."

"Tell you what," his father said, sitting down on the edge of Jordan's bed. "Why don't we make something fun for dinner tonight. How about we make Mom's favourite pizza?"

"The one with the pineapple, green peppers, and anchovies on it?" Jordan caught himself smiling in spite of everything.

"That's the one. And we'll make it together, just

like we used to," his dad said, grabbing one of Jordan's feet and tickling it.

Jordan screeched with laughter.

"Do you remember, your mom always used to make it when we'd had a bad day? She always knew best when it came to what was good for us."

"She sure did," Jordan said. Then added, "I really miss her, Dad."

"Me too, Jordie. Me too. But we're gonna be okay because we have each other." He ruffled Jordan's hair. "I'll meet you in the kitchen. We have a pizza to make."

"Sure. I'll be there in a minute."

As his dad left, Jordan picked up his phone and sent a text.

**I'm sorry about what happened with your dad. And I'm sorry about the way I reacted.**

He hit send, then sent another message:

Moments later his phone chirped with a text from Nathan:

# 20 The Bird and the Castle

ON MONDAY MORNING Jordan stood by Mr. Swan's counter in the Belvedere lobby. He checked his watch. It was exactly 7:30. Although classes didn't begin until eight, Jordan liked to get there early. Better early than late. It took fifteen minutes to get to school, assuming there were no delays.

Jordan checked to see if there was a text from Nathan. Nothing. Should he text him? No — that would look needy. He nervously tapped his fingers on the counter. Mr. Swan eventually put his hand on Jordan's, signalling that the tapping must stop. "If you go outside, maybe you can see your friend coming," he offered.

"Yeah." Jordan went outside and stood at the foot of the stairs. He stood for five minutes, then sat for five more. He caught his knee vibrating. *Where the hell is he?* Jordan stood and was about to text when he saw Nathan coming along the street, looking into his hands.

"Where have you been? We're going to be . . ."

Nathan looked up at him. In his hands he held a small yellow and black bird. "He hit a window. I couldn't just leave him there."

Jordan stared down at the injured, helpless bird and saw the look in Nathan's eyes.

"Come on. Bring him upstairs."

Jordan and Nathan skipped the elevator and took the stairs two at a time. They burst into the apartment. Jordan yelled, "Dad, we need your help."

Jordan's dad came out of the bedroom. He was dressed for work. "What's wrong?"

"Nathan found a bird that hit a window. We're not sure what to do."

Nathan held out his hands. The little bird lay there. They could see it was breathing in short, fast breaths.

"Is it dying?" Nathan asked.

"Here. Give it to me."

Nathan gently passed the bird to Jordan's dad who carefully examined the animal.

"I have a few things I'll need to try if I'm going to save this little fella, but it'll take some time. Perhaps it's best if you both go wash your hands and get to school."

As they ran to school, Jordan was distracted by the possibility that he would be late to class for the first time in his life.

Nathan said, "Do you think your dad can save it?"

"He knows what he's doing. He's a veterinarian. If anyone can save it, he can."

They reached the school just in time. Jordan was two steps ahead of Nathan all the way.

★★★

At lunchtime, Jordan met up with Emma and Nathan and they told her about what had happened with the bird. As they made their way down the hallway Mr. Jenkins walked by and said, "You three might want to go and check out the modifications to the book club room."

Without saying a word, they ran toward Mr. Jenkins's office. As they dodged around the other students who filled the hallway, Jordan spotted Yan and Jinx.

"Follow us," Jordan whispered, and the other two joined the race.

"Why are we running? Did you do something you shouldn't have?" Jinx asked Emma. "Cuz, if you did, I'm here for you."

Jordan looked over at Nathan, who smiled. "Told you he likes her," Nathan whispered.

When they reached the basement, they headed through Mr. Jenkins's office and saw the entrance to the old staff room. A beautiful, framed painting was fastened to the door. The painting was of a book, opened to the front page which said X-Libris.

Jordan turned the knob and the door opened.

What was, just the week before, a plain room with walls covered in paintings, was now a room that looked like it was right out of a castle.

The floor was covered in richly coloured patterned carpets and was furnished with fancy old upholstered chairs. Beside each chair was a small, ornately carved, wooden table. Along one wall was a huge bookcase.

"I'm sorry it's empty," a voice said from behind them, "but I thought you'd want to be the ones to decide what books went in it."

They spun around. The caretaker stood there with a mop and bucket in hand.

"Mr. Jenkins," Jordan gasped. "Where did this all come from?"

"You'd be surprised what you can find in the storage rooms of an old school."

"And the sign on the door . . . Did you paint it?" Emma asked.

"Yeah. It was a little rushed but —"

"It's amazing!" Jordan interrupted.

"It's . . ." was the only word that came out of Yan's mouth. He just stood there, mouth open, staring around the room.

"This is perfect," Jordan said. "As president of X-Libris, I would like to make you, Mr. Jenkins, an honorary member of the club. All in favour, say aye!"

All five members yelled out, "Aye!"

"But how do you get to be an honorary member when anyone can join?" Jinx asked.

"Don't spoil the moment, Jinx," Emma said.

"I am deeply touched," Mr. Jenkins said, "and I graciously accept. Sadly, I won't be able to stay. I have a leaky toilet in the boys' washroom on the second floor to deal with. By the way, the club needs to have a new staff supervisor since you aren't in the library activity rooms anymore. The principal suggested that I might want to take on the job."

The five students cheered.

Mr. Jenkins left the room and closed the door.

# 21 A Kaleidoscope of Butterflies

THE AFTERNOON SEEMED TO CRAWL ALONG and Jordan was relieved to reunite with Emma and Nathan after the last class of the day.

Jordan's phone chirped with a text.

**If Nathan is with you, will you bring him home? It's about the bird.**

"It's Dad. He was wondering if you could come home with me."

Nathan looked worried. "Is it bad news?"

"He didn't say."

"I gotta go. I hope everything is alright," Emma said, giving Jordan a hug. "See you guys tomorrow." She looked at Nathan, smiled and gave him a hug too.

They walked home, only stopping to pick up a paper. Just before they got to the apartment, Jordan looked at Nathan's worried face and said, "It *might* be good news." He looked around quickly then, seeing no one, put his hand on Nathan's back and gave it a rub.

"I know it's just a bird," Nathan said, "but lately little things have been really upsetting me, especially with all the stuff going on with my dad. It's kinda shaken everything up inside of me. So, thanks."

Nathan turned to Jordan and hugged him. Jordan didn't want that hug to end. Then, as Nathan was pulling away, Jordan couldn't be sure, but he thought he felt a light brush of something on his ear.

*Did he just kiss my ear?*

As they walked up the stairs Jordan took a deep breath. They entered the apartment and he set the paper down. "Dad?"

He was used to his father sitting in the living room, watching TV, or reading when he got home from school, but this afternoon his dad came out of his bedroom, closing the door behind him. Jordan tried to read the look on his father's face.

"I didn't realize it earlier, but you must be the friend who loaned Jordan that nice shirt," his dad said to Nathan.

"Yeah," Nathan replied, blushing slightly. The Nathan that Jordan knew up to this point would have talked up a storm.

"It's nice to see he's made a friend with such good taste. Maybe it'll rub off on him." Jordan's dad smiled and said, "Now, come on. Follow me." He headed back toward his room.

When they reached the closed door, Jordan's dad turned to Nathan and said, "He was in bad shape when you brought him in. Most of the time when a bird hits a window it breaks its neck because their bodies are so fragile."

Jordan felt Nathan move closer to him until they

were touching shoulders. He sensed Nathan was preparing for the worst.

"Luckily for you, he just had the wind knocked out of him," his dad said as he opened the door.

It was then that Jordan heard the bird singing. In the corner of the room, an ornate cage sat in the sun by the open window. The little bird that Nathan had handed over to Jordan's dad that morning, clinging to life, now clung to the perch and sang out to the world.

"So, it's going to be all right?" Nathan asked as he walked up to the cage and stared at the little bird.

"He might have come around on his own if you'd left him where you found him," Jordan's dad said, "but odds are, with all the hungry cats in this neighbourhood he probably would have been eaten. You saved him."

Nathan looked at Jordan and gave him a huge smile.

Jordan smiled back, then looked at the cage. He recognized it.

"Isn't that Mom's? The one from our old living room?"

"Yeah. I kept it. You kept her books and I kept her birdcage. It's the first time I've brought it out of the closet since we moved here."

Jordan gave his dad a hug. "She'd love that it was being used again."

"What do we do now?" Nathan asked.

"Well," Jordan's dad said, "I think we should let him go. Do you remember where you found him?"

"Yes," Nathan said. "There's a park nearby."

"Then lead the way. Let's set this little guy free," Jordan's dad replied.

They made their way down the street to the far end of the park, away from the roads and taller buildings. Nathan placed the cage on the ground and knelt beside it. The little bird hopped about inside, calling out *perchicoree, perchicoree.* He looked up at Jordan's dad who smiled and nodded his head. "Go ahead. I think he's ready."

Nathan opened the cage and the little goldfinch hopped up onto the door, cocked his head and looked up at Nathan, then flew up into the branches of a tree.

They stood and watched the bird for a moment before Jordan's dad said, "Well, boys, I guess our job here is done."

Nathan was watching the bird as it bounced from branch to branch. "I think I'd better stick around for a while and see how it's doing," he said.

"Jordan?" his dad asked.

"I think I'll keep Nathan company," Jordan said to his dad.

"I'll be off then. I'll pick up something for dinner on my way home. I'll keep it hot for you. Nathan, you're welcome to join us, if you'd like."

"Thanks, but I think my mom will have made something already."

Jordan saw his father smile, then he headed off in the direction of The Danforth, a street where every other door led into a restaurant.

★★★

After his dad left, Jordan and Nathan lay on the grass, looking up at the bird, who didn't seem to be in any hurry to fly away. It just perched there and sang louder than ever.

Jordan heard Nathan giggling. He turned his head and saw a kaleidoscope of monarch butterflies flittering about Nathan's head. There were no butterflies anywhere else. Nathan didn't seem bothered by them, or even surprised, although there had to be at least half a dozen of them flying around him or resting in his hair.

"They're beautiful," Jordan said softly, not wanting to scare them away.

"I think they're thanking me for saving their friend, the bird."

*Could he really believe that?* Jordan thought. Then he remembered his mother had told him that there was much more to nature than one would think, and it would always surprise you. At that very moment, one monarch left Nathan and flew to Jordan, landing on his left shoulder. Jordan felt a wave of love wash over him. He gasped, and all of the butterflies rose in the air and flew away.

Nathan and Jordan started to laugh and looked up

into the tree where they discovered that the goldfinch was gone.

Nathan slid his hand over and let his little finger touch Jordan's. Without thought, Jordan quickly slid his hand over Nathan's and held it tight.

"I remember my mom said that in literature butterflies represent the souls of the dead," Jordan said.

Nathan looked at him. "Maybe the one that flew to you was your mother's. I hope I have a soul that will come back as a butterfly."

Jordan knew that Nathan was serious.

"Jordan . . ." Nathan started, "can I ask you something personal?"

Jordan's heart flipped about in his chest. "Sure," he answered nervously.

Nathan paused. "You *are* gay, right?"

Jordan froze. The next thing he knew, he'd closed his eyes and said, "Yes."

"Good," Nathan said.

Jordan smiled and squeezed Nathan's hand. He wanted this moment to last forever.

# 22 Finding Sebastian

AFTER JORDAN HAD WALKED NATHAN HOME and had dinner with his dad, he went to his bedroom. He couldn't stop thinking about Nathan. The butterflies in his stomach were going crazy and he didn't feel in control. He needed to focus on a task. What could he do to distract himself?

*The school project!*

Jordan pulled out the coil-bound notebook that contained his hand-written copy of *The Swordsman's*

*Destiny.* He thought he should refresh his memory about how it compared to *Twelfth Night*. He looked up the story of the play online. It was a romantic comedy filled with mistaken identities and practical jokes. A girl disguised herself as a boy while she hunted for her twin brother, and there were two guys who *might* be in love . . .

*Two gay characters in Shakespeare?*

He got up from the bed and went to the Shakespeare section of the bookshelves. He ran his finger along the books and found his mother's volume of *Twelfth Night*. He carefully opened it, treating it like it was a valuable, rare book which, to him, it was. His mother had a habit of writing in the margins of her books. She made notes on just about every page. Jordan often found great hints here as to what stories were about. *Twelfth Night* was no exception.

As he leafed through the play, he came to act 2, scene 1. There was a section that she had highlighted. It involved the characters Antonio and Sebastian. In the margins she had written "Love." Then, in act 2, scene 3, he found a note in his mother's handwriting taped to the page. It had Jordan's name on it. He had never seen this before. He gently removed the note and opened it up.

> *If you've found this note, you are probably studying this play in school. I hope so. It's a beautiful story, and one you might relate to. I know that you've faced many challenges in life, but I know you. You will overcome them, especially if you find a special friend who will be there for you when you need it. Jordan, you will always be my little Antonio. I encourage you to go out there and find your Sebastian.*

# 23 In Search of a Hero

JORDAN WAS EXCITED about the first official X-Libris meeting in their new room. Everyone was talking and jumping around trying all of the chairs so that they could get the one that was right for them. Jinx and Yan flipped a coin over who would get the bright red and gold chair. They decided to make it the best two out of three flips. When it came down to the best three out of five tosses, they decided to alternate weekly, starting with Yan getting the chair this week.

The group was so delighted with the room that twenty minutes had passed before Jordan looked at his watch and realized he needed to take control. He cleared his throat. "I think it's important to discuss the group's English presentation. As we agreed, our project will be my story *The Swordsman's Destiny*. It has everything Miss Street could want. It's based on *Twelfth Night* and it's got the same characters but it's a bit more modern. My idea is to turn the story into something we can read out during the presentation."

Jinx put up his hand.

"You don't have to do that, Jinx. We're not in class," Jordan said.

Jinx lowered his hand and sat there quietly.

"Did you have a question?" Jordan asked him.

"Oh, yeah," Jinx said then shot up his hand again.

"Yes?" Jordan asked.

"Will I get to read a part?"

"There's parts for everyone."

"Oh," Jinx said, then sat silently before slowly raising his hand a third time.

"Yes?"

Jinx said, "I'd like a good part."

"They're all good parts. I thought we could read two sections of the story. In the first one, there's a character named Viola, who disguises herself as a boy."

"I'll read that part," Emma said.

Jordan continued, "Then there's the character Orsino who is in love with Viola."

"That sounds like a role for me," Jinx said, as he looked at Emma.

"Then, for the second half of the reading, there's Antonio, the hero, and Sebastian, his friend."

Emma said, "Since it's your story, Jordan you should play the hero and maybe Nathan could be your friend."

Everyone looked at Jordan. He felt a bit dizzy.

*You can't spend your whole life running from things . . .*

Jordan took a deep breath and said, "Okay."

"Is there something for me?" Yan asked.

Jordan was having trouble focusing. "Uh . . . the narrator. And they have the most words."

"I can do that," said Yan.

Emma grinned. "This is perfect. The teachers are going to love it."

Jinx, who Jordan had noticed stared at Emma every time she spoke, said, "Yeah. Everything Emma said."

Jordan looked over at Nathan, who was nodding his head. "It *is* perfect," Nathan said, "but I was wondering . . . Would it be *more* perfect if, rather than reading the story, we acted it out like a play?"

Everyone began talking at once. Everyone agreed — it should be done as scenes from a play. Everyone that is, except Jordan.

"It's too much. I don't think I can," he said, quietly.

"Come on, Jordan," Emma said. "Be brave. I'd love to see you as the hero."

Jordan felt panic rising. He remembered the kiss at the end of the story between Antonio and Sebastian. Reading the action aloud was one thing, but if they had to act it out it would mean he would actually have to kiss Nathan. In front of everyone. He didn't know how to explain his fear because no one else knew that was how the story ended.

Yan interrupted Jordan's thoughts. "If it's a hero you're looking for, Emma, I'll take the part and Jordan can be the narrator."

Emma looked at Jordan, who was having difficulty breathing. Before anyone could say anything else, the door opened, and Mr. Jenkins poked his head in.

"Sorry to disturb you, but I have an appointment to get to and I'll have to lock up in a few minutes."

"I think we're all done here, Mr. Jenkins," Nathan said.

Emma, Yan, and Jinx left, talking excitedly. Nathan stayed behind. He approached Jordan, who sat quietly in his chair.

"You okay? I hope you don't mind me suggesting acting out the story?"

"No," Jordan said. "It's a good idea. A really good idea."

"But . . ."

"I don't want Yan to play the hero. I want to read that part, but I don't know if I could act it out in front of the school."

Nathan gently rubbed Jordan's back in small circles. His breathing calmed.

"I'm sure Yan will do whatever part you say," said Nathan. "After all, it's your story. And, as for your fear of acting, I can help with that. Come with me."

# 24 Do You Trust Me?

NATHAN WALKED WEST from the school and then took a winding road down into the valley.

"Where are we going?" Jordan asked.

"You'll see."

Eventually, they got to a footpath that seemed to head off to the south. "This way," Nathan said and turned through a field of weeds taller than their heads and into a clearing surrounded by trees. The sounds of the city disappeared.

"What are we doing here?" Jordan asked.

"We, my friend, are going to find the actor in you."

Jordan stopped Nathan. "I'm not sure I can do this."

"What?"

"I'm not sure I can act out *The Swordsman's Destiny*."

"What are you most afraid of?" Nathan asked.

"There's a kiss at the end of the story between Antonio and Sebastian. I'm not sure if I can do that in front of the whole school." Jordan said this all very quickly, his face growing hot.

Nathan smiled at him. "Would you rather I kiss Yan at the end of the story?"

"No." Jordan hesitated. "I guess it's not just the kiss that scares me. It's that I'm not in control of how people will react. What if they boo, or yell, or . . . ?"

Nathan shrugged. "That's the point of acting it out — to make people feel something. And you can never control what other people feel."

"I don't like things being out of my control."

"Do you trust me?" Nathan asked.

"Yes," Jordan answered nervously.

"Just remember, you're safe here and nobody can see or hear you but me."

"Okay . . ."

Nathan got a sly grin on his face. "Do you like to sing?"

"No!" Jordan was horrified.

"Why?"

"I can't," Jordan protested.

"Everyone can sing. Some just do it better, that's all. Now, come on. Do what I do."

Nathan sang a scale. Jordan didn't know much about singing, but he could tell that Nathan was among the group that did it better.

"Now you try," Nathan said.

"No."

"Why not? No one can hear you out here."

Jordan opened his mouth a bit, then closed it. "No. I'm . . . too embarrassed."

"In front of me?" Nathan sounded disappointed. "But I thought you trusted me."

Jordan felt very uncomfortable. It was like his skin didn't fit right.

Nathan frowned. "Maybe this was a bad idea. You don't have to do anything you don't want to do." He turned and slowly headed toward the path.

Jordan could tell that Nathan was trying to help. Really help — not like others who said they wanted to help and just forced him to do things. He did what he never expected he'd do, standing in a forest in the middle of the city. "La, la, la, la, la, la, la," he sang, softly.

Nathan turned and smiled so widely, Jordan thought that Nathan's head would split open.

"That was awesome!"

"No. No — it was terrible."

"Don't you dare. You have a great voice. Try it again and, this time, if you're scared, just close your eyes. Pretend I'm not even here."

Nathan sang another scale. Jordan closed his eyes

and sang it back. It may have been a bit wobbly, but he made it through the scale.

"You see, you *can* do things you didn't think you could do."

"But it's just in front of you!" Jordan said.

"It's still a start," Nathan said. "You know that you can do it in front of me, and when you're comfortable with that, you can try it in front of X-Libris and by the time the presentation comes along you'll be able to do it in front of everyone."

"You mean singing?"

"I mean acting out the scene."

"You really think I can do it?" Jordan asked.

"It's not what I think that matters. If you're ever going to get past your fears, you need to do it for *you*. You have to do it because *you* want to, not me. If you can do that, I think you're going to be an amazing Antonio, and I'll be there for you, whatever you need."

Jordan stared at Nathan, stunned.

"Come on. This is getting way too serious." Nathan grabbed Jordan's hands and spun them both around until they dropped from dizziness.

Jordan lay beside Nathan, staring up at the sky. "This place is magical."

"I discovered it just after I moved to Toronto. I come here as often as I can. It's where I can let my imagination go wild."

"What do you imagine?"

"Sometimes that I'm alone on an island. Sometimes I'm a wild animal on the African savannah."

"Like a meerkat?" Jordan teased.

"No. A lion!" Nathan got up on his hands and knees and stalked around, roaring. He looked over and charged, positioning himself over a giggling Jordan. Nathan stopped, looking down at Jordan's face. He bowed his head slightly. Jordan's heart was racing. He watched as Nathan's lips parted. They were a beautiful shade of red, and full. Before he thought about what he was doing, Jordan lifted his head up and quickly kissed Nathan. With his head now safely back on the ground, Jordan was terrified that he'd made a bad decision and might have ruined everything. What he saw was Nathan, his wide eyes shining, and a huge smile on his face. Nathan slowly lowered his head toward Jordan and kissed him back.

Jordan's heart exploded into a thousand smiles. This felt so right, but it also scared him.

He rolled out from under Nathan. "What time is it?" Jordan asked.

"I don't know. Almost five I guess."

"I gotta get home. Dad'll be expecting me."

They got up and brushed themselves off. Jordan took his time, making sure every blade of grass and each fragment of leaf was removed from his clothes.

"So, how do you feel about acting out the part of Antonio now?" Nathan asked.

"Kissing you in the woods is a lot different than kissing you in front of the whole school. I'll have to think about it," Jordan said.

"While you're thinking about it, just remember this." Nathan kissed him one more time. "Now, let's get you home."

# 25 A Most Awesome Day

JORDAN OPENED THE DOOR to the apartment and before he could say or do anything his father called out, “Good, you’re home.”

It was then that Jordan realized that he had forgotten to pick up his dad’s newspaper. His heart sank. “Dad, I’m sorry. I forgot your paper.”

“The paper can wait. Listen, I’ve got something I want to talk to you about.”

“Okay.”

His dad continued. "That bird your friend saved, it got me thinking, about my work, about the animals. Jordan, I think it's time to get things back to more like they were."

Jordan paused before responding, "Okay. . ."

"I was wondering if you'd be all right with me heading back to work full-time? It would mean that I wouldn't be getting home until six or six-thirty, so you'll have to spend more time by yourself, or maybe with your new friend."

"Sure. I can do that," Jordan answered. Inside, he felt a small piece of his heart click back into the place where it used to be. "That would be nice," he added.

"By the way, I like your friend, Nathan. We should have him over for dinner sometime."

"That would be great."

"Speaking of dinner, what do you say that we treat ourselves to a meal out to celebrate everything? Maybe, pizza, or Greek food?"

"Indian food, I think," Jordan replied.

"Indian it is then. Let's go. I'm starving."

As they got ready to go to the restaurant Jordan texted Emma.

**Big news. Dad's doing a lot better. He's going back to work full-time.**

**Bigger news. Kinda freaked. I kissed Nathan.**

★★★

Family rules at dinner included, "No Devices At The Table," so it wasn't until after they'd left The Delhi Deli that Jordan saw he had thirteen texts from Emma, the last one being:

**You'd better be dead, cuz if you aren't I'm gonna kill you!**

He texted back:

**Out for dinner with Dad! Call you soon.**

As soon as he got back to his room, Jordan called Emma.

She answered with, "You had me worried. I thought maybe Nathan had kidnapped you or something, but then I thought: why would anybody want you, when you treat your best friend this way . . ."

"Hi, Emma. How are you?"

"Other than mad at you, fine."

"Please don't be mad. I had the most awesome day and I don't want it to end."

"So . . . he kissed you?"

"Better than that. I kissed him!"

"Oh my god!" she squealed.

"I know! I don't know why, but we were in the most romantic place and . . . it just happened. He has the nicest lips."

"I want the deets. Was it long and passionate? Was there tongue?"

"Ew, no. It was just a . . . a quick kiss."

"That's it?"

"I didn't know what I was doing. I've never done it before."

"You need to take lessons."

"I don't have to, because he kissed me right back. Twice. Soft, slow kisses —"

"Did he give tongue?" she interrupted.

"God, you're gross . . . A bit," he confessed.

A text buzzed on Jordan's phone. "I gotta go. Got a text from Nathan. See you tomorrow."

Jordan looked at the text.

So, now that we've kissed, does this mean we're going out? 😘

Jordan's heart fluttered. He typed back:

Yes 😘

Jordan froze as he saw the kiss emoji on his screen. Somehow the emoji made it more real. It made it more . . . permanent, like it could be used as evidence in court. His finger hovered over the screen for what seemed like an hour before he took a deep breath, closed his eyes, and pressed send.

# 26 Confessions

IT HAD BEEN TWO WEEKS since Jordan had started dating Nathan. Jordan had shared *The Swordsman's Destiny* with X-Libris and when Yan had found out that he would have to kiss Nathan if he played Antonio, he happily took on the role of narrator. Jordan and Nathan had worked together to turn his story into a script and today they had met on their own in the X-Libris room to stage the end of their scene.

After they had agreed on what it would look like,

Nathan asked, "Have you kissed many guys?"

"None, really."

"Does your dad know you're into guys?"

"I think so. We never really talk about it, but he did seem really happy when I brought you home, and I don't think it was just because of the bird."

Nathan laughed.

"Did your mom know . . . before she died?" Nathan asked.

"Yeah. I remember telling her I felt different. She smiled and asked me what I meant. I just said, "Nothing," and pretended I hadn't said anything.

"She asked me if I thought I was more attracted to boys than girls. I couldn't speak I was so embarrassed. My face must have turned a hundred shades of red. She said that there were lots of stories about men who loved other men, and lots of people in real life too. She told me it was perfectly normal. I remember that's what she called me: normal." Jordan smiled at the thought. "I think it was about that time that she read me *Twelfth Night*. And after that, I wrote *The Swordsman's Destiny*."

Jordan stopped and looked at Nathan. "I need to tell you something."

"You can tell me anything."

"You've probably noticed," Jordan began. "I can't stand when things are out of order or when people don't follow the rules. I'm afraid of a lot of things, because I always imagine all the things that can go wrong. And when I'm nervous I fidget like a five-year-old."

"But that's one of the reasons I like you," Nathan said.

"I need to tell you *why* I'm this way."

It all started to pour out of him. He couldn't stop it.

"Two years ago . . . before my mom knew she was dying, she'd been feeling sick. She was supposed to go to a doctor's appointment, but I was having a meltdown. I've always had them, they've just gotten worse. That day she stayed with me at home instead of going to see the specialist. And because she stayed home and missed the appointment, she couldn't get in to see the doctor for another three months . . .

That's when they found her cancer. She died a few months later. I think that, maybe, if it hadn't been for me, the doctor would have caught the cancer earlier and she'd still be alive. I think that because of me, she's dead." Jordan's body shook and tears streamed down his face.

Nathan hugged Jordan tight and held on for what seemed like an eternity. Eventually, he let go, looked at Jordan and said, "You can't let yourself believe that. Her cancer was probably already bad. She chose to stay with you that day because she loved you. I don't think you could have done anything that would have made her leave you alone."

Jordan's sobs gradually subsided.

Nathan continued. "I want you to know that I think you are amazing just the way you are, and we've all got things that we wish were different. Do you remember a few weeks ago, when I told you I was having problems with my dad?"

Jordan nodded.

"And I said he was getting remarried?"

"Yeah."

"Well, his new wife, she already has a kid. I looked them up on Facebook and Instagram. Her son's my age. And he plays hockey. I found one picture of him labelled 'Max and his girlfriend.' The only thing I could think was that my dad hated me so much that he left my mom and found someone else with a normal son. Not the little gay boy he already had. How messed up is that?"

"But you can't think that. I think you're totally perfect."

Nathan smiled and said, "Not everyone sees it that way."

"I guess we're both pretty messed up," Jordan said. "Maybe it's like my story. Antonio was fated to meet Sebastian. Just like I was fated to meet you. Maybe it's destiny."

Nathan smiled at Jordan and then gave him a kiss. Jordan felt himself blush and the heat rushed through his entire body. He was sure that Nathan could feel it.

Just then the door of the room opened, and the boys leapt apart. Mr. Jenkins came in with his coffee.

"How's the great play coming?" he asked.

"Just fine," Jordan and Nathan said in unison.

The caretaker walked to the back corner of the room where there was an easel covered with a sheet. He carefully removed the covering and pulled out his brushes.

Jordan asked, "Can we see what you're painting, Mr. Jenkins?"

"Uh, I guess. It's not finished, but . . ."

The boys walked around the easel and looked at the unfinished picture. Mr. Jenkins was painting the room as it was today, with its rich carpets and old chairs, and some of Mr. Jenkins's paintings replicated in their frames on the wall. However, in his painting, the walls were stone and twenty feet high with arched stained-glass windows. He had turned the old staff lunchroom into an ancient baronial hall.

"It's beautiful," Jordan said.

"This is how we first saw it," Nathan said. "We joke about it being our castle, and here it is, come to life."

Mr. Jenkins tried to suppress a smile. "You boys are far too kind."

Jordan looked closely and saw that Mr. Jenkins had started to rough in people sitting in the chairs. Jordan was there and so was Nathan. He pointed at them and looked at the caretaker.

"You've got us in there!"

"Only in rough. It will get better. I promise. And the others will join you in their seats."

"Mr. Jenkins — this is amazing!" Nathan shouted out.

"You five will live here forever in your castle for as long as this painting exists, symbols of perseverance, hope, and the love of books."

As they were packing up to go home Jordan saw Nathan working on an idea. He always got a slight crease in his brow and squinted his eyes when he was figuring something out. "Mr. Jenkins, could you do us another favour?"

"If I can."

"In the painting, would you include yourself, at your easel, maybe creating this painting? You're a member of X-Libris and can't be left out."

The old caretaker smiled and simply said, "I will. Thank you."

# 27 The Swordsman's Destiny

IT WAS THE DAY OF THE PRESENTATION. Since multiple classes were presenting, a special assembly had been called.

Jordan took extra time that morning getting ready. He brushed, then re-brushed his hair which refused to look neat. He decided to wear the sparkling dark blue shirt that Nathan had given him on the day of the cafeteria pizza fight. He thought it might bring him good luck.

While the second-last presentation took place, Nathan, who had taken on directing their project, called the group together.

They stood offstage, waiting for their introduction. Nathan gathered them in a circle.

"We're going to do great today. Just listen to each other and forget there's an audience. In the world of *The Swordsman's Destiny,* we are the only ones who exist. The audience are just the ghosts of the enemies we have vanquished, and they can do nothing to harm us."

*Nathan is already in character*, Jordan thought.

Then the voice of Miss Street came from the stage. "And finally, presented by the X-Libris book club, we have a dramatization of selections from an original work by Jordan Shepherd entitled *The Swordsman's Destiny*, inspired by William Shakespeare's *Twelfth Night*."

When Yan began his narration, Emma and Jinx made their way onto the stage.

As Viola, Emma wore a baseball cap that covered her long hair, and she was dressed in a bulky orange shirt covered by overalls. As Orsino, Jinx was wearing his newest sweater and his newest jeans. He wanted to impress Emma and the rest of the school.

At the appropriate moment, Viola said that she didn't feel like dressing as a man anymore, then took off the overalls and shirt and revealed a knee-length skirt and a bright red satin top. Someone in the audience whistled. Emma ignored it and kept going.

She passionately delivered her speech about how Orsino had said terrible things to her while she was in disguise. Jinx looked truly scared.

When Jinx, as Orsino, offered his speech of apology, and confessed his love for her, there was a chorus of boos from the audience.

Emma turned to the crowd and held up her hand. As Viola, she turned back to Orsino and said that she believed that anyone could change if they were given a chance, and that if Orsino truly felt sorry and promised to treat her with the respect she deserved, she would consider going out with him on a date.

A few people in the audience cheered at that.

Jinx decided to improvise and attempted to kiss Emma, but she quickly turned her face, so he only managed to kiss her on the cheek. The audience laughed.

Emma finished the scene by dragging Jinx off the stage saying, "I will teach you how to kiss properly, but not until you earn the right."

The audience applauded.

As soon as the applause had died down, Yan continued his narration, explaining that there was another set of characters in the story that needed to have their fate resolved: Antonio and Sebastian.

It was time for Jordan and Nathan to take the stage.

Jordan froze on the spot. Nathan stood beside him and said, "You'll be great. And you won't be alone. I'll be with you."

"I can't," Jordan said, petrified.

Nathan said, "Jordan, I'm here for you."

Jordan closed his eyes and took a deep breath. First, he focused on things he could smell: the sweetness of Miss Street's perfume in the distance; the scent of a dried-up orange peel somewhere near the edge of the stage; the rubbery scent of the gym mats piled against the side wall of the stage wings, and the smell of sweat that lingered on them.

Then he opened his eyes and focused on four things he could touch: the dusty surface of the stage curtain, the smooth texture of the wooden bench he was standing beside, and the softness of the shirt he was wearing, a shirt that Nathan had given him. The last thing he felt was the touch of Nathan's hand who had taken hold of Jordan's and was now staring him in the eyes.

"I'm here for you," Nathan repeated. "Together we can do this."

Jordan walked onto the stage and he could feel the blood pulsing in his temples so loudly that he was sure the audience could hear it. He looked out into the crowd of students sitting in the dark, watching. The auditorium was nearly full. He wanted to turn around and leave but Nathan had already begun the scene. He was lying on the stage, portraying the body of Sebastian who had washed ashore after a shipwreck.

Jordan knelt over Nathan's body and, as Antonio,

he picked up the wrist of his friend and felt for a pulse.

He wasn't sure what happened in that moment, but no matter how hard he tried, he couldn't find a pulse. For one horrible moment, Jordan thought somehow Nathan had actually died, and tears began to fall from his eyes. But what happened next surprised him. Instead of calling for help, Jordan spoke the lines of the story . . . words of confession of a love so deep that it hurt. He lifted Nathan in his arms and said that he would give anything for Sebastian to be alive once more.

The audience in the gym was still and silent. To Jordan, it felt like everything was happening in slow motion.

Jordan wept as he recited the lines he had written many years ago: "You can't be dead Sebastian, for you are my destiny."

It was at that moment that Nathan stirred. He winked at Jordan, lifted his head, and passionately kissed him on the lips.

The audience erupted. There were jeers (Jordan distinctly heard Brody shout out "Fags"), there were gasps of surprise, but mostly, there was applause which slowly grew louder and louder.

Jordan looked out and saw that Mr. Jenkins had risen to his feet, and that others were now joining him. Soon most of the audience was standing. At the back of the crowd, Jordan saw the principal hauling Brody out of the auditorium.

As Jordan and Nathan finished the scene, Emma and Jinx made their way onto the stage, and Yan joined them. They linked hands and bowed again and again. Jordan whispered to Nathan, "I think I'm in love with you."

Nathan smiled and said, "Me too."

The applause was still ringing in his ears as Jordan left the stage. Miss Street gave him a double thumbs-up. Jordan found his way into the back hall.

Then a strange thing happened. A good-looking student came up to them. Jordan recognized him as Tyler Cardy, the president of the student council and the most popular kid at school.

"You guys were great," he said then turned

to Jordan and Nathan. "You've got way more guts than me. And you," he turned to Emma. "You were incredible."

Jordan watched her and tried not to laugh. Her mouth had fallen open.

"Thank you?" was all she said.

Then Tyler asked, "Would you like to grab a cup of coffee sometime? We could maybe call it a date."

"That's so sweet but I already have a boyfriend," Emma said.

Jinx looked at her surprised and said, "You do?"

"It's you, you idiot," she said, putting her arm around Jinx's waist.

"Lucky guy," Tyler said to Jinx, then walked away.

Jinx looked even more confused than normal. "Wait. Does that mean . . . ?"

"I'll explain everything to you later," Emma said.

Probably the biggest surprise of all was that several kids came up to Jordan to find out how to join X-Libris. Somehow the book club had become popular.

# 28 What's Normal?

JORDAN WALKED NATHAN HOME.

"That was the greatest day ever!" Jordan said excitedly. "You were fantastic, by the way. Oh, and I heard that because of what he yelled out, Brody has to write out an apology then go from class to class and read it out loud to everyone."

When they reached Nathan's front door Jordan realized he hadn't shut up since they had left the school.

"I'm sorry. I haven't let you say a word."

Nathan laughed. "It's okay. I'm happy that you had such a great time."

"It was a-mazing." He paused then asked Nathan, "Why do you like me?"

Nathan thought for a moment before answering. "I like the way you're so tightly wound up. It's cute."

"Cute?"

"Actually, adorable is a better word."

"I'm a freak. Just ask anyone. Ask Brody."

"You think I'd take his word on anything?"

Jordan snorted. "Well, I'm not what you'd call normal."

"What's normal? Normal's boring. Normal's being like everyone else. It's . . . spaghetti without the sauce. You wanna be that?"

"It would be less exhausting," Jordan replied.

"Yeah, I guess it's easier to be like that kid in English class. The one in the third row by the window."

"And what's wrong with him?" Jordan asked.

"He picks his nose and eats it."

"Ewwwwww!"

"You wanna eat your own snot?" Nathan asked, before reaching out and tickling Jordan's ribs. He leaned in and gave Jordan a kiss. "I like you just the way you are."

They sat on Nathan's front steps for an hour, talking, before Nathan asked, Do you want to stay for supper? I know my mom would love to meet you," Nathan said.

Jordan paused. "My dad's expecting me home soon. . ."

"I understand." Nathan looked disappointed.

Jordan reached for his phone. "But I could text him and let him know that you asked, and I'm sure he'd be great with it."

Jordan tapped out a quick note to his dad. The phone pinged back with a message right away.

Sounds like fun. Look forward to hearing how the presentation went when you get home.

Jordan smiled at Nathan. "All good."

Nathan grabbed Jordan by the hand and started leading him to the front door, then stopped suddenly.

"So, now that it's okay for me to play your boyfriend on stage, can I play him in real life? In public?" Nathan asked.

"Yes," Jordan said. He kissed him again.

★★★

On his way home, Jordan thought about what had happened over the past few months. He had gone from being a loner, obsessed with order, and afraid of most things in the world, to having a boyfriend who *accepted* him as being obsessed with order, and afraid of most things in the world. He'd found someone who liked him for who he was, someone who had given him the strength to become who he wanted to be. He knew his dad and Emma accepted him, but this was somehow different.

Jordan took out his phone and opened up his contact list. The last of the three names was Nathan's. Jordan opened Nathan's contact information. At the bottom of the screen, he hit the star icon and added Nathan to his favourites. He was the only one. Jordan's heart fluttered.

As he walked up the stairs to his apartment Jordan thought about what Nathan had said about being normal, and he had a realization: he *wasn't* normal. He was himself, and for the first time in his life, he thought he might just be okay with that.

# ACKNOWLEDGEMENTS

I would sincerely like to thank the following people for their assistance in making Not Not Normal a possibility:

Allister Thompson for suggesting that I consider writing a gay love story for younger readers, and taking on the substantive edits of the manuscript;

Jennifer Rayner, educator and friend, who answered countless questions about what secondary school life is like in Toronto;

James Lorimer, Morgan Wright, Megan Kearns and Hanna Caunda for their detailed observations and editing work which made the book better.

Most of all, my partner in everything, Scott White. He is my first reader and story editor, patient interpreter of questions, handler of social media, and all-around calming presence in my life. Without him, nothing is possible.